To Debbie
from Cousin Charlotte 7/74

THE BOBBSEY TWINS'

ADVENTURES WITH BABY MAY

Baby May is stolen from the zoo! In a daring game of hide-and-seek the Bobbsey twins catch the thieves and rescue the little elephant as well as the treasure hidden in her bag of toys. At the same time, the young detectives find a missing friend and make her very happy.

THE BOBBSEY TWINS
By Laura Lee Hope

THE BOBBSEY TWINS OF LAKEPORT

ADVENTURE IN THE COUNTRY

THE SECRET AT THE SEASHORE

MYSTERY AT SCHOOL

AND THE MYSTERY AT SNOW LODGE

ON A HOUSEBOAT

MYSTERY AT MEADOWBROOK

BIG ADVENTURE AT HOME

SEARCH IN THE GREAT CITY

ON BLUEBERRY ISLAND

MYSTERY ON THE DEEP BLUE SEA

ADVENTURE IN WASHINGTON

VISIT TO THE GREAT WEST

AND THE CEDAR CAMP MYSTERY

AND THE COUNTY FAIR MYSTERY

CAMPING OUT

ADVENTURES WITH BABY MAY

AND THE PLAY HOUSE SECRET

AND THE FOUR-LEAF CLOVER MYSTERY

WONDERFUL WINTER SECRET

AND THE CIRCUS SURPRISE

SOLVE A MYSTERY

IN THE LAND OF COTTON

AT MYSTERY MANSION

IN TULIP LAND

IN RAINBOW VALLEY

OWN LITTLE RAILROAD

AT WHITESAIL HARBOR

AND THE HORSESHOE RIDDLE

AT BIG BEAR POND

ON A BICYCLE TRIP

OWN LITTLE FERRYBOAT

AT PILGRIM ROCK

FOREST ADVENTURE

AT LONDON TOWER

IN THE MYSTERY CAVE

IN VOLCANO LAND

THE GOLDFISH MYSTERY

AND THE BIG RIVER MYSTERY

AND THE GREEK HAT MYSTERY

SEARCH FOR THE GREEN ROOSTER

AND THEIR CAMEL ADVENTURE

MYSTERY OF THE KING'S PUPPET

AND THE SECRET OF CANDY CASTLE

AND THE DOODLEBUG MYSTERY

"Keep 'em up there!" Bert exclaimed

The Bobbsey Twins' Adventures with Baby May

By

LAURA LEE HOPE

GROSSET & DUNLAP
Publishers   New York

1971 Printing

PRINTED IN THE UNITED STATES OF AMERICA
LIBRARY OF CONGRESS CATALOG CARD NUMBER: 68–12753
The Bobbsey Twins' Adventures with Baby May

CONTENTS

CHAPTER		PAGE
I	MYSTERY BABY	1
II	THE SPY IN THE TREE	12
III	THE BLUE BAG	22
IV	YIPPEE FOR TIPPY!	31
V	LETTUCE ON THE ROOF	40
VI	A BOBBING LIGHT	49
VII	THE PINK FAKE	59
VIII	DROWNED BIKES	68
IX	THE CLUE IN THE MIRROR	78
X	A NOISY SHADOW	87
XI	THE CHASE	97
XII	THE TATTOOED COOK	105
XIII	A LAKE MONSTER	115
XIV	THE ANIMAL PRISONER	125
XV	A MUDDY RESCUE	134
XVI	BERT'S INVENTION	145
XVII	A SHAKY PERCH	154
XVIII	THE ELEPHANT'S TRICKS	164

THE BOBBSEY TWINS'
ADVENTURES WITH BABY MAY

CHAPTER I

MYSTERY BABY

"I CAN'T wait to see the new little elephant!" exclaimed six-year-old Flossie Bobbsey. She skipped into Pet Land with her blond twin, Freddie.

A smiling young woman in slacks waited inside the gate. She wore her red hair in a long, sleek bob and carried a camera over her shoulder.

"Hi!" she said. "I see you got my message."

"We came straight from school, Tippy," said Nan Bobbsey, who was twelve.

"Are you going to take our pictures?" asked Freddie.

"Yes," Tippy answered, leading them into the children's zoo. "Also, the elephant needs your help."

"How?" asked Bert, who was Nan's dark-haired twin.

"You'll see," said Tippy and added, "another thing. There's a mystery about this animal."

They rounded a clump of bushes. Straight ahead, at the foot of a wooded slope was a large wire pen with a long low shed at the back. A small elephant stood in the pen.

Nan gasped. "Look!"

A man in a checkered jacket was hanging by his hands from the edge of the shed's roof, his legs dangling inside the pen.

The children ran up to the fence. "What are you doing?" Freddie called.

The man twisted his head and gave them a wild-eyed look.

"What do you want in there?" Tippy asked sternly.

The intruder dropped to the ground. He turned and glared at them, red-faced. "Who are *you?*" he asked.

"I happen to be the official photographer for the Lakeport Zoo," said Tippy coolly, "and you have no business in that pen. Bert," she added, "would you please run for the manager?"

"No, wait!" said the man quickly. "I can explain." He smoothed back his limp blond hair. "I dropped an important paper and it blew in here. I couldn't find a keeper to get it for me, so I climbed in."

The children looked around the bare ground of the enclosure. "I don't see any paper," said Nan, "but we'll help you look for it. Miss Martin is going to take our pictures with the elephant."

Tippy took a key from her pocket and opened the padlock on a door in the end of the shed. She led the way through the dim shelter and out a wide center door into the pen.

"How big was the paper?" Bert asked.

"Never mind," the fellow muttered. He pushed past them into the shed.

Surprised, Bert and Nan followed. From the side door, they watched him stride up the hill. In a minute the checkered jacket disappeared among the trees.

"What do you think he was up to?" Bert asked.

"I don't know, but I see how he climbed onto the roof," said Nan.

She pointed to some wooden crates piled up against the back wall of the elephant's house. "He used those."

They went back into the pen where they found Tippy looking very thoughtful. The young photographer was the Bobbseys' new friend and neighbor. She lived alone, and the twins often visited her small house.

"I don't believe there was any paper," Tippy said.

"Neither do I," Nan agreed.

"Maybe the fellow is mixed up in the mystery you spoke of," said Bert. "Tell us about it, Tippy."

Just then Freddie called, "Come on, everybody!"

Flossie added, "Look at the elephant!"

They turned to see the small twins in the opposite corner of the cage. Near them stood the little gray elephant. Her head was down and the tip of her trunk rested listlessly on the ground. Between her front feet lay a dusty blue cloth bag.

"What's the matter with her?" asked Flossie.

"The zoo doctor says she's homesick," Tippy replied.

"Poor thing! She needs friends," Nan remarked as they crossed to her.

"I know you Bobbseys love animals," said Tippy. "I was hoping you could make her feel at home. Then maybe she will do her tricks and I can get pictures of them. The zoo in Bangkok told us she's a good performer."

"There was an article in the newspaper about her last night," Bert remarked. "It said she was a present from the children of the royal family of Thailand to the children of Lakeport."

"That was nice of them," said Flossie.

"Did we send them a present, too?" Freddie asked.

"Yes. An American buffalo," replied his brother. The Lakeport school belonged to a World Friendship Program and had sent gifts to children of several other countries.

"What's the elephant's name?" said Flossie.

"Supaje," replied Tippy.

"Hello, Supaje," said Flossie.

The animal did not move.

Tippy sighed. "That's how she's been all day. I was here when she came in the truck this morning. She won't eat or drink either."

"I think she should have an easier name," said Flossie, " 'cause she's only a baby."

"I agree," said Nan, and thought for a minute. "Why don't we call her May—because it's the month of May."

Flossie clapped her hands. "That's good! Baby May!" Everyone agreed this was a fine name.

"Now that that's settled," said Bert, "tell us about the mystery, Tippy."

"Someone tried to steal Baby May."

"Steal her!" the children exclaimed.

"When? Where?" Bert asked.

"In New York, night before last."

The photographer explained that the elephant had arrived by plane Saturday afternoon, two days before. "She was placed in the animal shelter at the airport to wait for her flight to Lakeport this morning.

"But Saturday night the keeper heard her trumpeting. He found two men climbing in the window high in the wall of her cage. When the intruders saw the keeper, they backed down. By the time he ran outside, the men were gone."

Bert looked puzzled. "How did they expect to escape with the elephant? The cage must be locked from the outside."

"It is," replied Tippy. "That's part of the mystery. The other question is why would anybody want to steal an elephant? It wouldn't be worth the risk."

"Maybe a circus owner," said Freddie, "because Baby May does tricks."

"Too dangerous," said his brother. "The airport's a busy place."

"Besides, the men must have known she would make a noise," Nan added.

"Maybe they were just robbers and climbed in the wrong window," Bert suggested.

"No," said Tippy. "The keeper heard one say, 'Are you sure this is the right elephant?' and the other one answered, 'Of course it is.'"

"I'll bet the man in the checkered jacket is mixed up with the kidnappers," said Nan. "Maybe he's one of them."

The others agreed.

"But certainly he didn't think he could steal the elephant from here in broad daylight," said Bert. "And how did he expect to get her out of this cage?"

"The whole thing doesn't make sense," said Tippy.

As she unslung her camera, two husky boys about Bert's age walked up to the fence. They were Danny Rugg and Jack Westley.

"Hi!" said Danny. "Can we be in the pictures?"

Tippy looked them over. "Maybe. Come on in."

The twins exchanged glances. Danny and his pal liked to make trouble for the Bobbseys whenever they could. While Tippy was getting her camera ready, the bullies swaggered into the pen.

"Why don't you ride on that elephant?" said Danny to Bert.

"Because she doesn't feel well."

Danny grinned. "You mean you're chicken."

"Sure he is," said Jack. "He's scared of a dopey-looking elephant that couldn't hurt a fly."

Danny sauntered up to Baby May. Before anyone could stop him, he scrambled onto her back.

"Giddap!" Danny shouted and kicked her. With a loud cry Baby May bolted!

"Cut that out!" cried Tippy. "Get off!"

But Danny hung on and the elephant did not stop until she reached a tub of water on the other side of the pen.

"Ride 'em, cowboy!" yelled Danny as Baby May dipped her trunk in the water.

The next moment the elephant's trunk curled above her head and she squirted water all over the bully!

"Help!" Danny yelled and tumbled off her back.

"You two ought to be ashamed," Bert said hotly.

Tippy pointed to the door. "Out!" she ordered, her green eyes blazing.

Sputtering, Danny got to his feet and the two boys ran off.

Tippy's face broke into a grin. "I got a wonderful shot of the shower bath," she said. "I'll send it to the newspaper."

The Bobbseys laughed. "Danny'll be furious," said Nan gleefully.

Head down, the elephant walked back to her corner. The children followed her.

"Poor Baby May," said Freddie, "let us pet you."

As he stepped closer to the elephant, she curled her trunk around the cloth bag, carried it to the opposite corner of the cage, and stood with her back to the visitors.

"What's in that bag?" Freddie asked.

Tippy shrugged. "Supaje had it with her when she arrived, and she won't let anyone touch it."

"I'll bet whatever is in there reminds Baby May of home," said Nan, "and she's afraid to let it out of her reach."

Just then Tippy smiled and waved to a short, bald man who trudged up to the cage with a pail.

"I brought our baby some milk," he said, walking into the pen. Tippy introduced the keeper as Mr. Henry.

"Glad to know you," he said, then put the pail

"Help!" yelled Danny

down in front of the elephant. "Now then, young lady, drink some milk!" But Baby May picked up her cloth bag and backed away.

Mr. Henry followed her. "Come on," he said loudly, "drink up! It's good for you!"

Baby May backed away again.

Nan spoke up quickly. "May I try, Mr. Henry?"

The keeper looked doubtful. "Well, all right," he said, "but be careful."

While the others watched, Nan stepped up to the animal and began to talk quietly. Coaxing and cooing, she moved the pail closer, then gently lifted the elephant's trunk and put it into the milk. Baby May started to drink.

While Tippy snapped pictures, keeper Henry beamed at Nan. "I have to hand it to you!" he said. "That's the first food she's taken today."

When Baby May had finished drinking, all the children began to pet her. She raised her head and looked at them shyly under her long lashes.

"How do you like that!" said the keeper. "No one else has been able to touch her."

Tippy told him about the intruder, and he promised to keep watch for the fellow. Taking the empty pail, Mr. Henry left.

As the twins waved to him, they noticed a balloon seller standing outside the cage. He was a tall man with thick black hair and heavy eyebrows. On his cart were bunches of colored balloons and souvenir canes. As he watched the children and the elephant he looked worried.

"I wonder what's the matter," Nan thought.

"Come on," said Tippy, slipping her camera into the case. "Let's call it a day."

After saying good-by to the elephant, they all left the cage. As Tippy padlocked the door, the balloon man was pushing his cart slowly away.

The twins walked with Tippy in the opposite direction and rounded the clump of bushes.

A minute later, shrill trumpeting split the air.

"Baby May!" cried Nan. "What's the matter with her?"

CHAPTER II

THE SPY IN THE TREE

THE twins and Tippy raced back toward the elephant cage.

A strange sight met their eyes! Baby May was walking beside the fence, dragging her cloth bag in the dust. Outside, the balloon man was running along in a crouch, making frantic stabs through the wire with the curved handle of a cane. It looked as if he were trying to hit Baby May's legs!

"Stop that!" Bert shouted as he raced toward the man.

Startled, the fellow dropped the cane, jumped to his feet and dashed up the hill. Bert sprinted after him. As he caught up, the man whirled and seized him by the shoulders.

"Nosey kid!" he hissed. "Mind your own business!"

With a savage push he sent the boy stumbling backward down the slope. Bert fell hard. Breathless but unhurt, he scrambled to his feet. The man was gone.

Bert returned to the bottom of the hill. The other twins, Tippy, and keeper Henry were in the elephant cage with a stocky man who had bristly gray hair. He was holding the balloon man's cane.

Tippy introduced him as Mr. Burns, the manager of the zoo. "I was at the llama pen with keeper Henry," he said, "when we heard the elephant's noise and came running."

Bert told his story and Mr. Burns frowned. "The fellow sounds dangerous." He glanced over at Nan, who was comforting the trembling elephant. "That young lady seems to have quite a knack with the animal," he remarked.

"Yes," said Tippy and told him that she counted on the twins to help make the elephant feel at home.

"We'd like to call her Baby May," Flossie piped up.

The manager smiled. "It's all right with me."

"Why do you think the bad men wanted to hurt Baby May?" asked Freddie.

"I don't know," the manager replied. "The balloon man applied for a job this morning and insisted on starting to work today. He gave his name as Jones. It was probably false."

Keeper Henry spoke up. "I told Mr. Burns about the man in the checkered jacket."

"Maybe he and the balloon man are the two who tried to kidnap Baby May in New York," Bert suggested.

"Maybe," said the manager. He looked puzzled as he stared at the cane in his hands. "But why should he try to hit her with this?"

"That stumps me," Bert admitted. "And I can't figure out why the other fellow wanted to get into the cage."

"Do you think the bad men will come back?" asked Flossie anxiously.

"I don't know," Mr. Burns replied, "but I'll have the night watchman keep his eyes open for trouble."

"And I'll get rid of the crates behind the shed so no one can climb up that way again," said Mr. Henry. He hurried off and the others also left the cage. As Tippy locked the door, Nan noticed the balloon cart some distance away.

"I'll have our zoo police pick that up," said Mr. Burns. "Maybe they'll find a clue to who the fellow is and what he was doing."

As they walked through the children's zoo, Flossie admired the colorful animal shelters. There was a blue castle on a hill for the goats, llamas, and deer that grazed on the fenced slope.

A white cottage surrounded by a picket fence housed a sheep family. Around the duck pond were trees and bushes. Amid them stood a small red pagoda.

"Everybody has a nice house but Baby May," remarked Flossie.

"She needs a new one," her sister agreed.

The manager escorted them to the front

entrance of the main zoo where Tippy's station wagon was parked.

"Ride home with me," she said to the twins.

The four children collected their bicycles from a rack marked "Bike Park" and loaded them into the station wagon.

As the young photographer drove through the evening traffic, Nan said, "It must be lots of fun taking pictures, Tippy."

"It is," she answered. "Especially of animals and children. The best one I ever took was of a tiny Mexican boy on a burro. I've entered it in the big Foto-Film contest."

Bert's eyes lit up. "I heard about that. First prize is a trip around the world."

Tippy smiled. "You know what I'd do if I should win? I'd take pictures of animals and children in every country and then I would have them published in a big book. Whatever money I made from it, would go to needy boys and girls."

"That's a marvelous plan!" said Nan. "I hope you win."

"Do you think you have a chance?" asked Flossie.

Tippy grinned. "Sure. About one chance in umpteen million." She explained that hundreds of good photographers would enter the contest.

"You're good too," Flossie said loyally.

When Tippy pulled into her driveway she thanked the children for helping with the elephant and asked them to come to the zoo the next day. They promised, then hurried across the street with their bicycles and down to their house, three doors away.

Mrs. Bobbsey let them in with a cheerful smile. She was a slender, pretty woman with a sweet face. "Supper's ready!" she said. "I hope you're hungry!"

During the meal the children told their parents all that had happened at the zoo. Mr. Bobbsey, a tall broad-shouldered man, agreed that the mystery was puzzling.

"Why would anyone try to steal an elephant, I wonder?"

A motherly-looking colored woman, Dinah, brought in a basket of hot biscuits. She and her husband Sam had worked for the Bobbseys as long as the twins could remember. Sam drove a truck for Mr. Bobbsey's lumber company and Dinah helped with the housework. They lived on the third floor of the Bobbsey house.

"An elephant!" Dinah exclaimed. "My, my, some folks'll steal anything!"

After supper the girls went to the kitchen where Nan fed Snap, the Bobbseys' shaggy white dog. Flossie gave Snoop, the black cat, his supper. Afterward the cat washed his paws and the white spot on his chest and ran off.

Snoop liked to be alone. At bedtime he went to his box beside the furnace in the basement, but

Snap followed Bert and Freddie to their room. When the boys were in their beds, the big dog flopped down on a rug at the foot of the beds.

In the middle of the night Bert and Freddie were awakened by a sharp bark. Snap was standing by the window in the moonlight, his ears up.

"What is it, old boy?" Bert asked. Snap growled. The brothers hurried to the window.

"I don't see anything," Freddie whispered.

"Let's take a look," said his brother.

Quickly the boys put on slippers and robes. Bert took a flashlight from the dresser and they went into the hall, followed by the growling dog.

Nan came out of the girls' room. "What's the matter with Snap?" she asked softly, tying the sash of her bathrobe. "I was awake and heard him bark."

"Maybe there's a prowler," Bert replied.

Holding the dog's collar, he led the way downstairs. Near the bottom all three stopped short as Snap growled louder. Someone was moving on the porch!

Was it the man who had pushed Bert down the slope?

As they stood frozen, a piece of white paper slid under the door.

"A note!" Nan whispered.

The children hurried down. Nan picked up the paper and unfolded it.

"This is from Tippy," she said, "and there's a key."

She read aloud: " 'Dear Nan, I have just had a phone call from my sister. She is very sick. I am driving to her house at once and will probably stay two weeks. Please go on working with B. May. Enclosed is key to my place. Would you mind keeping an eye on things for me? Thanks a lot and I will get in touch soon.' "

Snap gave a soft woof and Freddie patted him. "Everything's okay," he said. "It wasn't the bad man this time."

At breakfast Bert and Nan reported to their parents what had happened. Nan gave Tippy's key to her mother.

"I'm sorry to hear about her sister being ill," Mrs. Bobbsey said.

After school the twins rode their bicycles straight to the zoo. They left them in the bike park and hurried toward the elephant cage. On the way they all bought caramel corn. Freddie also got a small souvenir baseball bat.

As they entered Pet Land, the twins saw deer, goats, and llamas roaming loose among the pens.

The Bobbseys knew that the hoofed animals were sometimes turned loose to be fed and petted by the visitors.

The twins found Mr. Henry in the elephant pen. "There was more funny business with this animal last night," he told them as they entered.

"What happened?" asked Bert.

"A note!" Nan whispered

"The night watchman heard her trumpeting. I guess she scared the intruders away, because when he got here there was no one around. But he found tracks by the door."

The twins hurried outside. In a patch of soft earth they saw several long footprints and two short ones.

"These could have been made by the balloon man and the fellow in the checkered jacket," said Bert.

"If they meant to kidnap Baby May," Nan reasoned, "one of them would have had to bring a truck. The other must have hidden in here after closing time to open the gate."

"Let's check the back entrance for tire tracks," said Bert. "Come on, Freddie."

The boys started across Pet Land toward the rear gate which lay beyond the duck pond. The girls went back into the pen. Flossie told Mr. Henry about Tippy's going away.

"I know," he said. "She left a note for Mr. Burns, but no address. Tippy's taking her two weeks' vacation now. Too bad it has to be with somebody sick."

While Mr. Henry brought out hay from the shed, the girls fed caramel corn to Baby May. After a while Nan held out a handful and walked backward a few steps. The elephant picked up her blue bag and followed.

When Nan stopped, Baby May dropped the bag, and ate the candy. Nan did the same thing again, and the animal came for the snack, bringing the bag with her. With the candy for bait, the girls led the elephant around the pen.

"She'll do anything for caramel corn!" Flossie said.

Just then she glanced up at the slope and saw a bright flash of light. A moment later she spotted a patch of black-and-white-checked cloth high in a tree. "Look—the bad man!" Flossie exclaimed, pointing.

Nan frowned up at the wooded slope. "He's spying on us. I can see the sun flashing off his binoculars."

Quickly the girls told Mr. Henry. "There's a phone at the back entrance," he said to Nan. "Go dial zoo police. I'll stay here with Flossie and keep an eye on Baby May."

As Nan ran toward the gate, she suddenly realized she still had a handful of caramel corn. She paused and held it out to a nearby strolling llama.

"Hurry," she said. "Here's a treat."

The llama stepped over and its thick lips cleaned her hand. Close behind came others.

"Sorry!" said Nan, moving on. "It's all gone!"

The animals continued to nuzzle her hands and began to push one another. Goats and deer crowded close.

"Please!" she cried. "Let me through!"

Nan tried to run, but the animals pushed harder. With a cry she stumbled and fell!

CHAPTER III

THE BLUE BAG

AS NAN pitched forward, she fell against the soft back of a llama. The surrounding animals nudged and shoved, but Nan managed to get to her feet.

"Shoo! On your way!" came Bert's voice.

The herd scattered as he and Freddie pushed through, clapping their hands.

"Are you okay?" Freddie asked Nan.

"I'm all right," his sister replied. "They didn't mean to hurt me. It's just that they love caramel corn." Quickly she told the boys about the man in the tree.

The three hurried to the telephone at the gate and Bert reported to the zoo police.

"They'll be right over," he said to the others as he hung up. The children ran back to the elephant pen.

"It's too late," Flossie called. "The man's gone!"

"Maybe the police will pick him up," said Bert as they entered the cage.

Mr. Henry shook his head. "The zoo's big. There are many places to hide."

"Did you find any clues at the back gate?" Nan asked her brother.

"Just a lot of mixed-up tire tracks," said Bert. "That's a delivery entrance."

Flossie spoke up eagerly. "Guess what I can do? Look!"

She skipped over to Baby May and petted the elephant's trunk softly. Then Flossie stooped down, picked up the blue cloth bag and took a step away. Baby May turned her head to watch, but made no move to take the bag back.

"Why, Floss, how wonderful!" Nan exclaimed.

At that moment two policemen in gray uniforms hurried up to the fence and Flossie put down the bag. The children and Mr. Henry went over to point out where they had seen the man in the tree. As the officers headed up the hill, the keeper went back to his work in the shed.

"Let's see what's in the bag," Freddie said eagerly.

The twins returned to the elephant. Flossie knelt beside the bag and opened the drawstring. While Baby May watched, the little girl reached in and pulled out a cloth doll dressed in a colorful Thai costume.

"Isn't she pretty!" Nan exclaimed.

Then Flossie took out a brass bell with an

ebony handle. While the others passed these things around, she brought out a red rubber ball trimmed in gold, and a clothesbrush with a carved ivory handle.

"These must be Baby May's toys," Nan guessed. "I'll bet she uses them in her tricks."

"There's something else in here, too," said Freddie. He pulled out a small bag made of brown material. Inside it was a box covered in beautiful blue-green silk.

"What a yummy color!" Nan said. "What's inside?"

Freddie opened a little catch and raised the lid of the box. He pulled out a gold-colored cup. An elephant was outlined on it in sparkling green stones.

Bert gave a low whistle. "That's really beautiful!"

"All these things are fancy," said Flossie, "but this is the prettiest of them all."

Freddie grinned. "How do you like that? An elephant that has her own drinking cup!"

"You must remember she's a royal elephant," Nan said, "and she's used to the best of everything."

Carefully the children returned the toys to the bag, and Flossie put it between Baby May's feet. Just then the keeper came out with a long hose.

"We know what's in the bag, Mr. Henry," Freddie said. "Toys. You want to see them?"

"Sure I do." The keeper put down the hose

"That's really beautiful!" Bert said

and walked over. As he reached for the bag,
Baby May snatched it up and ran away. The
little man hurried after her. "Come on now!" he
said loudly. "Let me look, too!"

Baby May turned and trumpeted angrily.

Mr. Henry stopped and grinned. "It looks as
if the Bobbseys are the only ones who are al-
lowed to take it away from her!"

Shaking his head, he picked up the hose and
began to put fresh water in the elephant's tub.

Meanwhile Freddie took the little bat from
his back pocket and held it out to Baby May.
"Let's teach her to play baseball," he said.

After touching the bat several times, the elephant curled her trunk around it.

"Now go like this, Baby May!" said Freddie.

The boys pretended to bat baseballs. Suddenly
Baby May got the idea! Back and forth she
swung her trunk with the little bat held upright.

Quickly Bert took the red ball from the bag of
toys. He pitched it gently, so it hit the bat just as
Baby May swung. The ball sailed across the
cage!

Freddie whooped with joy as he leaped to
catch it. "That's great!" he cried.

While the boys played with the elephant, the
girls hurried away to a refreshment stand and
bought soda pop for all. Mr. Henry beamed
when the girls gave him one of the cold drinks.
As they crossed in front of the cage to reach the
boys, Baby May struck the ball hard.

"Watch it!" Bert yelled.

Nan jumped back. *Smack!* The ball hit a bottle she was carrying and it sailed out of the pen.

"Over the fence!" Freddie shouted. "A home run!"

Nan giggled and said, "No, Freddie, a pop fly!"

They all laughed and Bert said, "She should be called Baby Ruth instead of Baby May."

"All you have to do," said Freddie, "is yell, 'A home run!' "

Instantly the elephant swung the bat.

Bert chuckled. "No more today, Baby May!"

The girls went out and Nan found the ball. Flossie picked up the bottle and threw it in a nearby trash can.

When they returned to the cage, Freddie said, "Let Baby May keep the bat." Nan put the new toy and the ball into the bag, which she placed at the elephant's feet.

After drinking their soda, the children said good-by to Baby May and Mr. Henry. Outside they dropped their empty bottles into a can and hurried toward the front gate.

When the twins reached the house, they found there had been no word from Tippy that day. After supper Bert picked up the newspaper. Suddenly he grinned. "Look at this!" He held up a picture of Danny being squirted by Baby May.

The others laughed and Freddie said, "Boy, is Danny going to be mad!"

"Tippy must have dropped the picture off at the newspaper office last night on her way out of town," Nan said.

Bert continued going through the paper. Suddenly a small story on an inside page caught his eye. As he read it, his eyes grew bright with excitement.

"I knew it!" he exclaimed. "Listen to this, everybody!"

The family looked over and Flossie turned down the television set.

"What is it?" Freddie asked eagerly.

"Wait'll you hear this news!" Bert said.

He read them an article about a precious gold cup stolen the Friday before from the royal palace in Thailand. *On the cup was an elephant outlined in emeralds!*

"That's Baby May's cup!" Nan exclaimed.

"Of course! Don't you see?" said Bert. "The fellow in the checkered jacket and the balloon man must have stolen the cup. Then they hid it in the elephant's toy bag to smuggle it out of Thailand and into America."

"And now they're trying to get it back again," said Nan.

"But we caught the man in the checkered jacket before he could take it out of the bag," Flossie said.

Freddie spoke up excitedly. "The balloon man wasn't trying to hit Baby May. He was using his cane to hook the bag!"

"And those men won't give up," said Bert. "They'll keep trying to get their loot."

His mother nodded eagerly. "You're right."

Mr. Bobbsey strode to the telephone. "I'll call the police. They must pick up the cup right away before the thieves do."

"Oh, Daddy, ask the chief to let us get the toy bag," Nan pleaded.

"Baby May won't allow anybody else to touch it," put in Flossie.

Mr. Bobbsey smiled as he dialed headquarters. "I'm sure a couple of big strong policemen could get it away from her."

"But they'll frighten her, Dad," Nan protested. "And we're trying to make her feel at home."

"All right," said Mr. Bobbsey. "I'll see about it."

After talking to the police chief for a few minutes, he hung up. "Bert and Nan, you go with the officers," he said. "The chief will alert Mr. Burns."

Seeing the sad looks on the faces of the little twins, he patted Flossie's shoulder and tousled his small son's hair. "They don't need all of you. Let the older ones do this job."

Five minutes later two policemen called for

Bert and Nan in a patrol car. One was their friend, Howard Lane. He introduced the other as Officer Brown.

"The elephant pen is close to the back gate," Bert remarked as the car started off.

"Yes, but that's the long way around," said Officer Lane. "Besides, there's construction on Broad Street, so we'd also have to detour. We'll make better time if we head straight for the front gate."

In a short time he reached the zoo. Mr. Burns was waiting to let them in. The twins and the three men hurried past the dark cages.

Drawing close to Pet Land, the children began to run. They were first to round the clump of bushes and see the elephant pen. It stood empty in the moonlight.

Nan gasped. She and Bert ran to the side of the shed. The door stood open. The elephant was gone!

CHAPTER IV

YIPPEE FOR TIPPY!

"WE'RE too late!" Nan called as the policemen and Mr. Burns ran up to the empty shelter.

"Maybe not! Try the back gate!" cried Bert.

Hoping to catch the kidnappers, he raced off. He sped past the sheep cottage and around the duck pond, with the others at his heels. The back gate stood open. The twins dashed through it.

"There they go!" Bert cried. A small, closed black truck was just rounding the bend in the road.

The policemen rushed up with Mr. Burns. "Did you get the license number?" asked Officer Lane.

Bert shook his head sadly. "No sir. I didn't have time."

Nan pointed to the ground. "Look!" she said and picked up several kernels of caramel corn. "Now I know how they made Baby May go with them. They used our trick."

"But the men were after the cup," said Officer Brown. "Why take the elephant?"

"They *had* to," Bert said. "She would make a big fuss if they tried to take the bag away from her."

Mr. Burns spoke up. "I'm wondering where the watchman is."

The five began searching for him. While the officers beamed their lights behind the big rocks in the goat pasture, Bert and Mr. Burns checked the bushes around the pond. Meanwhile, Nan heard loud *baas* and saw that the sheep were moving restlessly in their pen.

"What is the matter with them?" she wondered.

She went through the wooden gate and crossed the yard. Peering into the dark cottage, she heard a groan. In a corner she made out the figure of a man!

"Come quick!" Nan called to the others.

In a few minutes the officers had carried the watchman into the open air. With their help he got to his feet. He said that he had seen two men sneaking up to the elephant cage. When he called to them to stop, they turned and ran over to him.

"Quick as a wink, the tall one knocked me down. I hit my head and went out like a light. They must have dumped me in the sheep house then."

"How'd the men get in the zoo?" asked Officer Brown.

"Same as last night," guessed Bert. "One

stayed hidden at closing time and later opened the gate for the other."

Mr. Burns nodded. "Probably the man in the checked jacket opened it. My police couldn't find him anywhere."

"We'll radio the alarm right away," said Officer Lane. Then Mr. Burns took the watchman home. One of the policemen drove the children to their house and the other stayed at the zoo.

When Nan and Bert broke the news to the younger twins, Flossie's eyes filled with tears. "Poor Baby May! We have to rescue her!"

"Yes, and that cup too, before the men manage to sell it," said Mr. Bobbsey.

Next morning dawned gray and dreary. After breakfast the twins sadly watched a television newscast asking all citizens to be on the lookout for the two men, the elephant, and the small black truck.

When the children left the house for school, they saw Danny Rugg leaning against a tree at the curb.

"I'm going to get even with you for that picture in the paper!" Danny yelled. "You'll be sorry!" He ran off.

At noon there was no word of the missing elephant. After school Bert and the girls hurried home, anxious for news. There was none. Freddie, who had stopped to play, came last. As he passed Tippy's house, a boy was ringing the doorbell.

"That lady's not home," Freddie called.

"I have a telegram for her," the boy replied. "The telegraph company's been trying to reach her by phone, but there was no answer so they sent me to deliver the message." He slid it partway under the door and hurried away to his bicycle.

When Freddie told his mother, she sent him back to get the telegram. Returning, he found Mrs. Bobbsey and the other children in the kitchen with Dinah. The cook had placed a big bowl of molasses cookies on the table with glasses of cold milk.

Mrs. Bobbsey thanked Freddie and took the telegram from him. "I think Tippy would want us to open this. It may be urgent. I'll inform the sender that she's away."

She opened the yellow envelope and read the telegram. "How wonderful!" she exclaimed. "Tippy has won first prize in the Foto-Film contest!"

The children cheered.

"Oh, that's great!" Nan exclaimed. "Now she can make her big book of pictures."

"A trip around the world!" cried Freddie. "Yippee for Tippy!"

"Yippee for Tippy!" Flossie repeated and giggled happily.

"Wait! There's more!" said their mother. "Tippy has to claim the prize by next Wednesday midnight or it will go to the runner-up."

"That's just a week from today," Bert remarked. "I hope we hear from her soon."

Talking happily of Tippy's good luck, the children ate their afternoon snack. As Flossie was wiping her mouth, the doorbell rang.

Bert answered it. His best friend, Charlie Mason, stood on the porch. He was a good-looking boy with dark hair.

"Hi!" said Charlie breathlessly. His brown eyes were snapping with excitement. "How would you like to go ghost-catching?"

Bert grinned. "It sounds great. Come on in!"

As Charlie stepped into the living room, the other children appeared from the kitchen.

"I was just over to the gas station and had air put in my bike tires," Charlie said. "Ed Evans was there helping out. You know, he's from the high school."

Bert nodded and his friend went on, "Ed's grandfather lives in a cottage down by Stony Creek. Last night he heard loud weird noises in the woods." Charlie grinned. "The Evanses know it isn't a ghost, of course, but Ed said that's what it sounded like."

While Charlie had been talking, the same thought had hit both Bert and Nan.

"Listen," said Bert eagerly, "Black Bear Woods runs down behind the zoo to Stony Creek. Suppose the kidnappers backtracked and took Baby May there. That would explain how they vanished so quickly!"

"They might be hiding her in the woods," Nan added.

"That's smart thinking," said Charlie, who knew about the twins' interest in the elephant. "Let's round up a search party. You come too, Flossie and Freddie! Get your bikes!"

"I'll call Nellie!" Nan suggested. Nellie was her close friend.

"Good," said Bert. "The more help the better!"

In a few minutes Nellie Parks arrived on her bicycle. She was a pretty girl with long dark-blond hair. She was wearing blue pedal pushers and a matching sweater.

As the searchers pedaled toward the zoo, Charlie suddenly chuckled. "I can just see Danny's face if we should find that elephant." He added, "Danny and Jack were getting air in their tires, too. They heard me tell Ed that I was going to ask you to investigate the noise. Danny said we were jerks to go looking for a ghost."

Bert grinned. "I don't care what he said as long as he doesn't try to come along."

About twenty minutes later the children cut into a shady side street. At its end they made a turn onto a dirt road which ran between the zoo fence and the woods.

At the back gate of Pet Land, Bert dismounted and examined the road where it started downhill into the forest. He spotted a pair of tire tracks and told the others.

"Let's follow them on foot."

The children quickly stowed their bicycles under some heavy bushes beside the zoo gate. Then they hurried down into the woods.

Excited at the thought of finding Baby May, they hardly noticed how overcast the sky had become. But the deeper the children walked into the woods, the darker it became. Far off there was a rumble of thunder.

"It's spooky," Flossie said.

Nellie giggled. "This is called Black Bear Woods. Are there any bears down here?"

"Of course not," said Charlie in a superior voice. "They were only here in pioneer times."

Freddie looked worried. He was walking last and thought he heard twigs cracking among the trees behind him.

The little boy hastened forward to Bert. "Wait a minute. I thought I heard a noise."

"Come on now," said his brother. "Quit your kidding."

"No, I mean it!"

The children stood still and listened. Silence.

Nan smiled. "Don't worry, Freddie. All the bears are in the zoo."

The children started down the hill again.

"We *hope* they're in the zoo," Freddie muttered, as he trotted close to Bert.

A few yards farther on, the road became rocky and the tire tracks vanished. The searchers stopped again.

"I thought I heard a noise," Freddie said

On either side of them was a narrow path. Bert wondered if the men had unloaded the elephant here and taken her to a hiding place.

"If they did, where is the truck?" asked Nellie.

"This road goes down to the creek and follows it out to the highway," Bert replied. "The truck must have gone that way."

"The brush is broken around the path on both sides," Charlie observed.

"Yes," said Bert. "That makes me think they unloaded the elephant here. If I know Baby May, they probably had a struggle with her."

"How can we tell which way they went?" asked Nellie.

Nan suggested that the search party divide up and examine both paths. The boys started one way and the girls the other.

As they walked deeper into the woods, the light grew dimmer. The wind moaned through the trees and the branches thrashed to and fro.

Suddenly they heard a banging noise ahead. Just then Nellie clutched Nan's sleeve.

"Look there!"

Amid the trees was a small shack.

Bang!

"That's where the noise is coming from," Nan whispered.

Flossie shivered. "Maybe the ghost is in there!"

CHAPTER V

LETTUCE ON THE ROOF

"YOU know there are no ghosts, Flossie," said Nan. "Maybe Baby May is in that shack and she's making the noise. We'll take a look."

"One of the men may be with her," Nellie whispered. "We'd better be careful."

"I know," said Nan. "Flossie, you stick right behind us."

The little girl nodded and shivered as the wind howled and the banging noise came again. Quietly the girls moved up close to the shanty and began to circle it. Reaching the back, they stopped short.

"There's our ghost!" Nan exclaimed.

Most of the wall of the shack had been broken out and the boards were scattered around. One still hung loosely in place. As the wind blew, it banged against another board.

"I'll bet Baby May was here and kicked her way out," Nan said.

The one-room shack was a shambles. A

wooden table lay beside a smashed chair. Broken crockery had spilled out of a fallen cupboard.

"Here's some caramel corn," Flossie said, picking up a bit. "That means Baby May was here."

The girls searched for the toy bag, but it was not in the shack.

Nan looked around at the wreckage. "I think maybe those men tried to take the bag from her and she broke away from them."

"If she still has it, the men will be after her," said Nellie.

Flossie looked tearful. "Oh dear! We just have to find her before they do."

Nan nodded. "I'll get the boys," she said, and hurried away.

For a while Nellie and Flossie poked around the shanty. They found some old newspapers and a rusty can opener.

"I don't think anybody has lived here for a long time," said Nellie.

The two wandered outside and sat on a log to wait. The wind had died down, but the woods seemed darker than before. After a few minutes, Flossie looked over her shoulder uneasily.

"What's the matter?" Nellie asked softly.

"I thought I heard somebody whispering," Flossie replied in a little voice.

"It's just the wind," said Nellie, but she glanced over her shoulder, too.

"I wish Nan and the boys would come back,"

Flossie said. "I have a creepy feeling somebody is watching us."

Nellie put her arm around the little girl. "Don't be afraid," she said. But she had the same uneasy feeling herself.

A few minutes later Nan and the boys arrived breathless. Bert and Charlie took a quick look around the shack.

"Come on!" said Bert. "Let's see if we can find Baby May!"

The trail was easy to follow, for the elephant had no path to use. Broken branches and crushed shrubs led the searchers downhill to a narrow dirt road bordering a wide creek. On the bank were big muddy prints showing that Baby May had stopped to drink.

As the children followed the tracks along the shore, Bert suddenly said, "Wait a minute!" They all stopped. "Listen!"

"I heard it too," said Nan softly.

A long, low moan came from the woods beside them.

"I told you something was following us," said Freddie.

Quickly Nellie and Flossie reported the whispering they thought they had heard. "Maybe it's the bad men," the little girl added.

A moment later the weird sound came again, followed by a telltale snicker.

"Danny and Jack!" said Bert in disgust. "Wouldn't you know?"

"Pay no attention to them," said Nan. "Maybe they'll go away."

Pretending not to hear the moans, the search party went on and followed the tracks along the stream. Soon they came to a cottage set in a clearing at the edge of the woods. In the yard near the trees were three low platforms with a large wooden box on each.

"The man keeps bees," said Bert, crossing the road to look at them.

"I hope they won't sting us," Freddie said.

"If you don't bother them, they won't bother you," Nellie told him.

A muffled snort of laughter came from the woods. The children exchanged looks.

"Okay, Danny! Come on out!" Bert called.

Instantly a long stick was thrust through the bushes. It knocked one of the hives off the platform. As the nest hit the ground, a swarm of angry insects poured out.

"Run!" Nan cried, and the children raced down the road with the young twins screaming.

"Ouch!" cried Charlie and slapped at his forehead.

At the same time several loud yelps came from the woods. When the children had left the bees behind, they stopped, panting.

"What a mean trick!" Nan exclaimed.

"Come back here!" roared a loud voice. They turned to see a white-haired man in front of the cottage. "What do you think you're doing?"

"Run!" Nan cried

The children went back, watching out for the bees.

"We're sorry," Nan said to the man. "But it wasn't our fault."

He continued to glare at them. The other children chimed in to explain what had happened, though they did not mention Danny and Jack by name.

Gradually the man grew less angry, and finally he sighed. "Sounds to me like you're telling the truth," he said. "I'll get you some ointment for that sting," he added, looking at Charlie. "Anybody else need it?"

The other children chorused "No" and thanked him. The man went into the cabin and returned in a few moments with a white tube.

As Charlie put salve on the red lump, he grinned. "I'll bet our two friends could use some of this."

Charlie returned the tube and thanked the man. Then the children told who they were and what they were doing.

The man looked interested. "So all the rumpus was made by the stolen elephant," he said. "I heard about the animal on television, but that idea never occurred to me. I'm Ed Evans," he added. "Your friend Ed's grandfather. He's named after me." Mr. Evans told them there were more houses farther along the road and suggested that they ask at them about the elephant. The children thanked him and offered to help put back the fallen hive.

"No, thanks," Mr. Evans said. "I'll do it. You go on about your business."

With Bert leading, the searchers picked up the elephant's prints on the bank. After a while the tracks led into the woods, then returned to the creek, farther along. The trail went back and forth several times.

"Baby May must have spent the night this way," said Bert. "She probably went into the woods to sleep but then heard people coming. Then she'd walk to the water and go on a little way."

Often the tracks led in circles among the trees. The searchers plodded on.

Meanwhile, the storm clouds had blown over. Pale sunshine was breaking through when the children came to three cottages facing the creek. The first had a screened porch. On the mailbox was the name Ford. A small woman in a pink cotton dress was trying to mend a tear in the screen.

Flossie's eyes were on the roof. "Look, everybody!" She pointed.

On it lay a head of lettuce!

As the children walked over to the woman Freddie ran ahead. "Hello!" he said. "Mrs. Ford, do you know there's a head of lettuce on your roof?"

The woman looked up and pushed back her

fluffy brown hair. She smiled and sighed. "Yes, and would you believe the lettuce was thrown there by an elephant?"

"Oh, wonderful!" exclaimed Nan. "That's the elephant we're looking for."

The woman looked puzzled. "What do you mean?"

"She was stolen from the zoo," Bert spoke up. "Didn't you hear about it on television?"

Mrs. Ford shook her head. "No, my dear. My husband and I just got back from a trip. We've been riding on the train most of the day. We haven't seen or heard the news.

"But an hour ago there was a noise on the porch. We came out and saw a little elephant push her trunk through the screen, reach in, and raise the hook on the door. Then she pulled out her trunk, slipped the tip into the handle, opened the door and came in. Believe me, we were too surprised to move!"

"My, Baby May is smart!" Flossie exclaimed, her eyes sparkling.

"And then, if you please," Mrs. Ford went on, "that elephant went over to a carton of groceries which had been left at the door and politely helped herself. She ate part of a loaf of bread before we worked up nerve enough to shoo her off the porch."

"Oh, I hope you didn't scare her," Nan said.

Mrs. Ford laughed. "Scare *her!* No, my dear, she scared us. After all, we had no one to help us.

It's early in the season and the other two cottages are still empty." Then she added, "We threw the lettuce to keep her from coming back onto the porch."

"And then she tossed the lettuce on the roof?" Freddie asked.

Mrs. Ford nodded. "Yes, I think she was kind of upset about being chased, but we managed to get her into the garage."

"Oh please, let us see her!" said Nan.

"She's gone now," was the reply. "We turned her over to the detectives."

Bert looked surprised. "The police were here?"

"Two plainclothesmen," Mrs. Ford replied. "One was tall, the other wore a checkered jacket."

CHAPTER VI

A BOBBING LIGHT

THE children groaned in dismay.

"Those weren't detectives," Nan explained.

Flossie added, "They were the elephant-nappers!"

Nan introduced the search party to Mrs. Ford. She called her husband, a thin man wearing glasses. The children told the couple about the theft of the cup and the elephant.

"Did Baby May have the toy bag with her?" Bert asked. Mrs. Ford nodded.

Mr. Ford spoke up. "After we got the elephant into the garage, we were going to call the police to come for her. But just then those two fellows came walking up. They said when they saw the lettuce on the roof and the torn screen, they guessed the animal was here."

"The men told us they had been searching the woods on both sides of the creek all day," Mrs. Ford added. "I think that last part was true, because they looked pretty tired and scratched."

"One man left but returned shortly with a small black truck," her husband went on. "They probably had it parked in a clearing up the road."

Bert sighed. "It's too bad you didn't know they were the thieves."

"They seemed all right," said Mrs. Ford. "One flashed a badge, but neither of us got a close look at it."

"That was probably a toy badge," said Freddie. "I have two—a policeman's and a fireman's."

Nan asked, "Did the men say anything that might give us a clue to where they were going?"

"No," Mrs. Ford replied. "But after they coaxed the elephant into the truck with caramel corn, I heard the tall one say, 'This baby's smart. A circus would pay a good fat price for her.'"

Flossie looked sad. "Poor Baby May! Maybe they'll sell her."

While Mr. Ford telephoned a report to the police, the older children boosted Freddie onto the porch roof. He tossed the lettuce to Mrs. Ford, then Bert helped him get down.

When Mr. Ford came outside, he offered to drive the search party to the zoo to pick up their bicycles. The twins accepted and piled into a station wagon standing near the garage. Mr. Ford drove up the bumpy road through the woods. On the way, he told them that the police captain had said he would alert circuses and carnivals in case the thieves tried to sell the elephant. The children got out at the back gate of the zoo, and thanked Mr. Ford.

"Okay," he replied. "Better luck next time!"

As the twins pedaled off, Freddie said, "Wow, it's late! We'd better hurry."

When they reached home, Mrs. Bobbsey looked relieved. "Where have you been?" she asked. "We've been keeping supper warm for you."

As they ate, the children poured out the story of their afternoon's adventure. "No wonder you are late!" exclaimed Mrs. Bobbsey.

"That was good thinking, Bert," said his father. "Not everybody would have connected the ghost with the elephant."

Mrs. Bobbsey smiled. "And now Daddy has a surprise for you."

Flossie skipped over to her father and sat on his lap. "Oh please, Daddy, what is it?"

"I'll tell you after supper, my little fat fairy!" Mr. Bobbsey said. Flossie grinned. She liked this pet nickname her father had given her.

"Will you tell your little fat fireman, too?" asked Freddie, climbing onto the arm of his father's chair.

The small boy loved fire engines and wanted to be a fireman when he grew up.

"Of course," Mr. Bobbsey said with a chuckle, "but first you must eat your vegetables and drink all your milk."

When the children finished, Mr. Bobbsey leaned back in his chair and said, "The surprise is that we are taking a trip this weekend."

"Where?" the twins chorused.

"To Footprint Lakes—in the northern part of the state."

"Yeah! Great! Super!" the four children cried out. Then Freddie added, "That's a funny name."

His mother explained that there were five lakes, each shaped something like a human foot. "We're going to the largest—Big Pine."

"When do we leave?" Bert asked.

"Day after tomorrow—Friday," said Mrs. Bobbsey.

On the way to school next morning the twins met Nellie and Charlie and told about the trip.

"Great," said Charlie. "I wish I were going."

When they reached the schoolyard Nellie giggled and said, "Look at Danny and Jack."

The bullies were leaning against the building. Each boy had a red lump on his face.

"Hi, fellows!" said Bert. "Where did you get those bee stings?"

"We don't know what you're talking about," Jack said sullenly.

Bert's eyes glinted with mischief. "Oh, I get it," he said. "Those are not bee stings. You've just got a bad case of hives."

Danny grew red in the face. "You think you're smart!" he sputtered. "You'll be sorry!"

Bert chuckled.

When the twins went home to lunch, it was drizzling, so they put on raincoats. By the time school was out the rain had become a downpour and deep water raced in the gutters.

Freddie and Flossie ran ahead, shouting and splashing happily. As they dashed onto their front porch, Dinah opened the door and Snap ran out, barking.

"I heard you coming," Dinah said. "Land sakes, you sure are wet!" Water was streaming off the young twins' coats and hats.

Freddie opened the mailbox and took out a letter. "It's for all of us—from Tippy."

"Be careful!" his sister warned. "You're dripping on it."

As Freddie shook the envelope, Snap leaped up, grabbed it, and raced across the yard.

"Snap! Bring that back!" Freddie exclaimed. He and Flossie scampered off the porch after the dog. Still playing, Snap ran to the curb.

"Put that down!" Freddie cried.

Flossie grabbed the dog. He barked and the letter fell into the racing water. Freddie dashed along the curb, trying to catch it. Finally he managed to seize the envelope.

"Is it all right?" Flossie asked anxiously as she ran over to him.

Freddie held out the soaked paper. "All the writing's washed off the front," he said.

Nan and Bert came up the walk. "What've

"Snap! Bring that back!"

you got there, Freddie?" his brother asked.

The little boy explained and Bert groaned.

"Oh, Snap, you're a naughty dog," Nan said to the pet, who was frisking around their heels.

"It wasn't his fault," Flossie said. "He thought we were playing."

The children took the envelope into the house and showed it to their mother. The letter inside was a blur of blue ink.

"There's not one word left," Nan said. "Did you see the return address, Freddie?"

"No, I didn't have time."

"Look at the postmark," Mrs. Bobbsey suggested.

Bert made a face. "It's all chewed up, except for a little corner." He peered at it. "All that is left are the letters of the state—Tippy's still in our state," he added.

The children and their mother looked worried. "How will we ever find her?" asked Flossie.

"We just *have* to find her, or she'll lose the prize she won," Nan said. "Maybe Dinah knows where Tippy's sister lives."

The others followed Nan to the kitchen and she asked the cook.

Dinah looked doubtful. "All I remember is that her sister's name is Margery. She's married and lives at a lake, but I sure don't know the name of it. Miss Tippy gave me a lift home from the market one day and told me about her sister."

"Thanks, Dinah. That's some help," said Bert. "Maybe Mr. Burns knows this Margery's last name." He telephoned the zoo manager, but he could not help. Neither could the newspaper, nor several of the neighbors.

"Mother," said Nan, "I think we should go over to Tippy's house and see if we can find her sister's name and address."

"That's a good idea," Mrs. Bobbsey agreed. "I'll get my raincoat and boots."

Five minutes later the twins and their mother trooped onto Tippy's porch. Mrs. Bobbsey unlocked the front door. They all took off their boots and walked into the dim living room. Bert switched on a light.

"Probably Tippy has an address book," said Mrs. Bobbsey.

She opened a tall desk in the corner. With Nan's and Bert's help she searched each drawer and cubbyhole, putting things back neatly. They found no clue to the sister's name or whereabouts.

Nan noticed a large picture album on a table and began to leaf through it. Suddenly she exclaimed, "See what I've found!"

Nan showed the others a photograph of Tippy and an older woman who looked like her. The two were standing in front of a small excursion boat with the name *Sea Sprite* on the bow. Underneath the picture were written the words, "Visiting Margery."

"That's a good clue, Nan," Bert said. "Now we have to locate the lake where there is—or was—an excursion boat by that name. It shouldn't be too hard to find Tippy's sister then."

"Maybe she lives at one of the Footprint Lakes!" Freddie put in excitedly. "We can look for her this weekend."

"That's right!" said Bert. "We'd better borrow the picture. It might help." His mother agreed. Nan carefully slipped the snapshot out of the album and Bert put it in his pocket.

As the Bobbseys were leaving, Flossie hung back. She had noticed a large yellow flower pressed and framed under glass, hanging on the wall. Beneath the dried bloom were printed the words, "M's Mum—First Prize." Below it was some small handwriting which Flossie read hurriedly as she followed after the others.

That evening the children gathered at the television set and watched the newscast eagerly. They hoped for news of Baby May, but there had been no trace of the missing elephant.

"I hope those men aren't being mean to her," said Flossie, looking worried.

Bert remembered how the balloon man had threatened him. "He's dangerous," the boy thought.

At bedtime Bert went out on the porch to whistle for Snap. The rain had finally stopped and large puddles gleamed in the street light.

Bert glanced toward Tippy's house. A light suddenly appeared in a window, then vanished.

"That looked like a flashlight," Bert thought. "Maybe it's a burglar." He was about to call his father, then decided to check first. "To be sure I'm not seeing things."

A few minutes later Bert slipped into Tippy's yard. He hurried to the rear and stood beside a big, sweet-smelling lilac bush. The light was moving past a window!

"Someone has a flashlight, all right," Bert thought.

The next moment he heard a door opening. As the beam came outside, he dived under a bush. Water dripped down the neck of his jacket, but he hunched his shoulders and made no sound. Bert's heart began to pound as the light bobbed straight toward his hiding place.

Suddenly the branches were thrust aside and Bert was yanked out by the collar!

CHAPTER VII

THE PINK FAKE

"ALL RIGHT, you! What are you doing in—" The gruff voice stopped short. "Why, it's Bert Bobbsey!" The blinding flashlight was lowered.

"Officer Lane!" Bert exclaimed. Though he was still dazzled by the glare, he recognized the policeman's voice. "I saw your light and thought you were a burglar."

The policeman chuckled. "That's what I thought you were. I heard you hit the bush."

He explained that one of Tippy's neighbors had seen a light in the house that afternoon. The neighbor knew that the photographer was away because the station wagon was gone. "The lady couldn't make up her mind whether to call the police or not," the officer said. "She wasn't sure whether the light had been turned on by a friend or an intruder. Finally she had her husband phone us a little while ago."

Bert laughed. "I can explain the light she saw." He told the policeman how and why the Bobbseys had searched Tippy's home. "Maybe the police could help us find her sister," he added.

"Without the lady's last name it may be hard," the officer said. "But we'll do what we can."

As they walked toward the street, the officer said, "Did you hear about the truck?"

"No. You mean the black one the thieves used?"

"Yes," the policeman replied. "A patrol car found it about an hour ago on the riverbank several miles from here. We know it's the right one because there were bits of hay and caramel corn inside. It had been stolen, of course."

"I wonder what those men have done with the elephant," Bert said. "If they sell her, I'm afraid we'll never get her back. We probably couldn't prove she was Baby May. I guess one elephant looks pretty much like another."

The policeman nodded, and Bert asked, "Do you think the thieves will try to sell the cup around here?"

Officer Lane shrugged. "So far we haven't heard that it was offered to any shopkeepers."

Bert asked if the zoo police had reported finding anything on the balloon cart.

"There were fingerprints," Officer Lane replied. "We checked them through the FBI and

got the results this morning. The tall fellow
is Harold Crow, a jewel thief. He usually
works with a partner named Fred Lester."

"I'll bet that's the fellow in the checkered
jacket," said Bert.

The officer agreed. Then he said good night
and headed for his car, which he had parked a
few doors down the street.

When Bert reached his yard, he whistled for
the dog. Snap came trotting up and the boy led
him around to the back porch. As if by magic
the cat appeared on the railing. "You come in,
too, Snoop," Bert said. "One lost animal is
enough to worry about."

Inside the lighted kitchen the other children
were having a bedtime snack of apples and milk.
While Bert told about meeting Officer Lane, the
girls wiped off Snap's and Snoop's wet paws
with an old towel.

"We heard about the truck on the nine o'clock
news while you were gone," said Freddie.

"With the alarm out, the men had to get rid of
it," Nan said. "I don't think they'll dare travel
with Baby May now."

"I wonder if they have been able to take the
cup away from her," said Freddie.

"I don't know," Flossie said. "Anyway, an elephant is an awful big thing to hide."

But next day there was no news of Baby May.
After school the twins found the family station
wagon in the driveway with the luggage for

their trip to the lake already in it. They said good-by to Dinah and Sam in the kitchen.

"If Tippy should call, Dinah, will you be sure to find out where she is?" Bert asked. "And tell her she won first prize in the contest."

"We will, honey," said Dinah.

Sam spoke up. He was a thin, friendly man.

"You young folks just forget about your two mysteries for a while. Go and have fun."

"We will send you both postcards," Flossie promised. "And Snap and Snoop, too."

That evening they ate supper at a highway restaurant. While Mr. Bobbsey paid the bill, Flossie went to the souvenir counter to buy cards.

She heard a little girl walking nearby say, "The elephant was near Freetown." The child was going out the door with a woman.

"Wait!" cried Flossie. But the two were already outside and more people were coming in.

Flossie squeezed past a stout woman and out the door. The child was getting into a car in the parking lot with her mother.

"Wait a minute!" Flossie called, waving at them. But they did not notice, and a moment later the car drove away.

Disappointed, Flossie walked back to the restaurant. She met the other Bobbseys coming out and told them what had happened.

"We have to go through Freetown," said her father. "You can watch for the elephant."

"Wait!" cried Flossie

"Do you think it was Baby May, Daddy?" Freddie asked as he climbed into the car.

"It's possible," his father said, "but don't count on it."

"Maybe the bad men got another truck and brought her out here and then she escaped again," said Flossie hopefully.

"After all," Freddie remarked, "there can't be a million elephants around." The others laughed.

As it was growing dusk, Mr. Bobbsey cut off the highway onto a winding road. "We're getting near Freetown now," he said.

Flossie pressed her nose tighter against the glass and almost held her breath. Suddenly they rounded a bend and saw a huge pink elephant sign! White lights advertised a highway store.

Flossie gave a cry of disappointment and Freddie exclaimed, "It's a fake!"

"That's too bad," their mother said kindly.

On the other side of Freetown, Mr. Bobbsey turned onto a long driveway. All the children perked up. Ahead of them was a log lodge with an iron lantern lighting the porch. A sign said *Big Pine Hotel*. The family left the car in the parking lot and carried their bags inside.

"Let's look around," Freddie suggested.

While their parents went to the desk, the twins gazed about the lobby. In the center was a colored poster showing a number of dancers in Thailand costumes.

"They're going to be here tonight," said Bert.

"Maybe they knew Baby May in Bangkok!" Nan exclaimed. "It would be fun to ask them tomorrow."

Next morning Freddie awoke early. Bert, in pajamas, was looking out the window. The little boy padded sleepily over to his brother. Below lay a wide blue lake sparkling in the sunshine. Dark green pines ringed the shore.

Freddie frowned. "I don't see any excursion boat."

"The lake curves down at the far end," Bert said. "The boat could be around the bend."

Cottages were scattered along the opposite side.

"Maybe Tippy's sister lives in one of those," Freddie said hopefully.

Bert nodded. "Let's go down to the lobby and see what we can find out about the boat."

Quickly the two boys dressed and took the elevator to the main floor. They hurried over to the desk. The clerk, a tall young man with black hair, looked up from the keys he was sorting. He smiled and said, "What can I do for you boys?"

Bert asked if an excursion boat named the *Sea Sprite* ran on the lake.

"No, there's no excursion boat here."

Freddie looked disappointed, but his brother went on, "Maybe there used to be one?"

"I wouldn't know," the clerk said. "You see, this is a new hotel and most of us who work here are strangers in these parts. You'll have to ask somebody who has lived around the lake awhile."

Bert hesitated, then took out the photograph. "Have you ever seen the older lady in this picture?"

"No, I haven't." The clerk smiled and added, "What are you fellows, anyway—detectives?"

"That's right," Freddie spoke up. "We're trying to find somebody."

"Sounds like you haven't got much to go on. Suppose I ask some of the guests about it? They might be able to help."

As the boys thanked him, the elevator door opened and their sisters came out.

"Mommy and Daddy will be down soon," Flossie announced. "We called their room on the telephone. Oh!" she said suddenly, looking straight ahead.

At a picture window stood a tiny young woman in an Oriental dress. Her black hair was drawn back tightly and twisted into a high knot.

"She's just like a little doll!" Nan whispered.

"Let's talk to her," Flossie suggested.

The young Thai woman heard them and turned, smiling. "Hello," she said. "My name is Thiang. What are yours?" Her voice had a sweet, musical twang. While Nan introduced the children, Flossie admired Thiang's dress. It was bluish-green silk with a slit part way up the leg.

The little woman smiled. "I am one of the Thailand dancers. This is a Thai dress. Do you like it?"

"Bee-yoo-ti-ful!" Flossie exclaimed. "It's the same color as the box Baby May's cup is in."

The dancer looked puzzled. "What cup?"

"She means the royal cup from Thailand," Nan explained. "The one with the elephant outlined in emeralds."

Thiang looked surprised. "You children have seen that? Then you must have been in Thailand!"

"No. The cup is here," Bert replied. "Haven't you heard?"

The children told her about Baby May, whose real name was Supaje, and the two thieves.

As the little dancer listened, a frightened expression appeared on her face.

"The cup was stolen?" she exclaimed.

Nan looked at her anxiously. "Yes. What is the matter?"

"I think I know where it is," Thiang whispered.

CHAPTER VIII

DROWNED BIKES

FOR a moment the twins were speechless with surprise.

Then Nan said, "Where is the cup, Thiang?"

"It may be in my brother's hands," she replied, looking worried.

The children were puzzled. "How did he get it?" Bert asked.

The little dancer seated herself in a large chair beside the window.

"My brother Sarad is a member of our troupe," she began. "We tour all over the world. One of Sarad's hobbies is the collecting of art objects that came from Thailand." She explained that fine carving and weaving were done in her country. "Besides, many beautiful things are made of gold and silver. Some look like lace."

"I remember—that's called filigree," remarked Nan. "We learned about it in school."

Thiang told them that there had been a story in a New York newspaper not long ago about her brother.

"Yesterday he had a phone call from a stranger who wanted to sell him something precious from Thailand. The man would not say what it was."

"Didn't your brother guess it was the royal cup?" Bert asked.

"No. We didn't know that it had been stolen," the dancer explained. "Sarad and I are the only members of our company who speak English, but we do not read it easily, so we seldom buy newspapers. We've been so busy with rehearsals lately that we have had no time to listen to radio or television."

"Where is your brother now?" Bert asked quickly.

"He went to meet the man who telephoned," the dancer replied.

"Where?" asked Nan.

"I don't know. He mentioned the call to me just before the performance last night. Afterward I forgot to ask him about it. He left early this morning."

"He can't be going too far away, or he would have told you," Nan reasoned.

"That is true. I am sure he expects to be back for this evening's show. But I am afraid," Thiang added with a little shiver. "If the object for sale is the royal cup, Sarad will recognize it, and guess it is stolen. If he acts as if he's suspicious, the men may harm him."

Nan felt sorry for the dancer. "Don't worry. I am sure he will come back safe and maybe have the cup with him."

"He might even know where the men went, so we can find Baby May," said Freddie hopefully.

Nan asked Thiang if she had ever seen the elephant perform in Thailand.

"Yes. Many times. I knew her trainer."

"Was Baby May happy there?" Flossie asked.

"Of course. She had the best of everything. You should have seen the house she lived in! It was red with a golden roof that curved like this." With graceful fingers she made a peak like those the children had seen on pictures of the temples in Thailand.

"No wonder Baby May is homesick," Nan said. "She probably misses her pretty house."

"Did she do many tricks?" Bert asked.

Thiang nodded. "Yes, she is very bright and had a wonderful trainer. It is most remarkable for such a young elephant to learn all that she has."

"Can she sit up?" Flossie asked.

"Oh, yes," Thiang replied. "The trainer just chirped or whistled to make her perform."

Nan's eyes sparkled. "Oh, Thiang, could you teach us the signals? Maybe we could make her perform for us when we find her."

Thiang glanced around the empty lobby. Then she leaned forward and taught the twins to trill and chirp and whistle as the elephant trainer had done for each trick.

"You have learned quickly," said Thiang warmly. Suddenly she raised a dainty finger. "I have an idea! How would you like to help at our performance tonight?"

"We'd love it!" Nan said as the others eagerly added, "Yes."

Thiang smiled mysteriously. "Then later today, I will have a surprise for you."

At that moment Mr. and Mrs. Bobbsey came out of the elevator. The children introduced the dancer to their parents. She made a tiny bow and, after talking politely for a few moments, excused herself and left.

The Bobbseys went to the hotel dining room. At the breakfast table the twins told their parents what they had learned from Thiang.

Mrs. Bobbsey looked worried. "Sarad might be meeting with the thieves right this minute!"

"Maybe. But we're not sure it was the elephant cup the caller was offering for sale," Bert remarked.

Mr. Bobbsey advised the children not to become excited. "When Sarad gets back, we will hear his story."

"Anyway, we have to look for Tippy's sister," Nan reminded them.

"Why don't you all take bicycles and ride

around the lake?" Mrs. Bobbsey said. "Daddy and I are going to play golf."

While the girls changed to pedal pushers and sweaters, Mrs. Bobbsey ordered a picnic lunch for the four children.

When they came downstairs, the desk clerk handed a basket to Nan and said, "You can pick up bicycles at the sports shed in the rear of the hotel."

Ten minutes later the twins were riding along a narrow road which circled the lake. A light wind ruffled the blue water, and the smell of pine was in the air.

Soon they came to a white cottage and Nan said, "It looks empty."

Nevertheless, Bert dismounted and knocked on the door. There was no reply. At the next three houses, it was the same story.

By noon they had circled halfway around the lake. Most of the cottages were closed. The few people they met knew nothing about the *Sea Sprite* or a woman named Margery.

Pedaling round a clump of trees, the children saw a log cabin facing a willow-shaded dock. An elderly man in dungarees and a straw hat was getting into a rowboat.

"Wait!" Freddie called.

The children placed their bikes beside the bushes and ran to the dock. Bert asked the questions and showed the photograph.

The man shook his head. "There's no excursion boat here. Never was one. I'm a real old timer, so I know."

The children's faces fell. Bert put the picture back in his wallet.

Freddie sighed. "I'm awful hungry and thirsty," he said. "Let's have lunch soon."

"Eat here if you like," the man said. "I'm going fishing." The twins thanked him, then he tapped a finger to his hat brim and rowed off. Nan went to her bike and brought back the picnic basket.

Seated on the shady dock, the children enjoyed cheese sandwiches and cold milk from a Thermos. For dessert they had fresh pears and chocolate cupcakes. Afterward, Nan put their trash into a refuse barrel next to the back door of the cabin.

Flossie skipped ahead to the road. Suddenly she called out, "Come quick! The bikes are gone!"

The others hurried to the clump of bushes where the bicycles had been left.

"Where can they be?" Nan asked, puzzled.

"Maybe somebody moved them for a joke," Bert suggested.

The twins searched up and down the road for a distance, but did not find the bicycles.

"Someone must have them!" Nan exclaimed.

Seeing broken bushes, Bert went through the opening and the others followed. They came out onto a large flat rock at the edge of the lake. Flossie glanced into the shallow water.

"There they are!" she cried. "Somebody drowned our bikes!"

The twins pulled the bicycles from the lake and dragged them back to the path.

"I'd like to catch whoever did this," said Bert, as he dried off his bike with a handkerchief. But as the twins pedaled back to the hotel, they passed no one.

After turning in the bicycles, the four children walked around to the front of the hotel. A stout woman wearing a flowered dress was seated on the porch. She waved to them. "Are you the detectives?"

"Yes," Bert replied, and the children walked over to her.

The woman smiled. "The clerk was telling me about you. I thought you'd like to know that there is an excursion boat at Fun Lake. I think it is called the *Sea Sprite.*"

"That's a wonderful lead!" said Nan. "Thank you for telling us."

"We'll check up on it as soon as we can," Bert promised.

Cheerful over the new clue, the children hurried upstairs.

"We haven't been to Fun Lake for a couple of years," said Bert. "I forgot about the boat there."

"I did too," said Nan.

"Somebody drowned our bikes!"

As the girls walked into their room, Nan gave a cry of delight.

Flossie exclaimed, "How bee-yoo-ti-ful!"

On her bed were four beautiful Thailand costumes, one for each twin. Pinned to the pillow was a note from Thiang inviting the children to wear the native dress while handing out programs before the performance.

Flossie called the boys, who were amazed at the black silk trousers and yellow jackets which had been left for them.

Bert grinned. "These sure are nifty."

Nan picked up the telephone to thank Thiang, but the operator told her that the dancers were not to be disturbed until after the performance.

"We'll have to put on these clothes right after dinner," Bert said.

It seemed to Flossie that the time would never come. When the girls finally were dressed, they looked in the mirror, and Flossie exclaimed, "I can't believe it's us!" Her gown was blue with a high collar, and Nan's was a shimmering green.

Their mother smiled. "You both look beautiful," she said.

Eyes sparkling with excitement, the four Bobbseys reported to the ballroom. The doorman beamed and gave each one a batch of programs. In the center of the room was a round platform and circling it were rows of gold-colored chairs. Soon the audience began to arrive. Almost everyone had a smile for the twins.

Finally the lights dimmed and cymbals clashed. A brilliant light bathed the platform, revealing a dancer with a sword. Spellbound, the audience watched the performers go through the dramatic dances. The Bobbseys kept wondering which was Sarad. And had he gone to meet the thieves? Did he have the cup?

As soon as the performance was over, the children hastened to the dressing rooms at the rear of the ballroom. Nan knocked at the door marked "Women Performers."

It was opened at once by Thiang. Her eyes were filled with tears.

"Sarad has not returned," she said.

CHAPTER IX

THE CLUE IN THE MIRROR

"NOT returned!" Nan repeated in alarm.

"Something has happened to my brother," said the dancer. "He would never miss a performance if he could help it."

Bert looked sober. "We must find out where he went. Perhaps he jotted down the address somewhere."

"Let's look in his bedroom," Thiang suggested.

Still wearing her makeup and costume, she led the children up the back stairs of the hotel to the third floor, where the dancers had their rooms. She opened a door at the end of the hall.

"This is Sarad's," she said. It was a small, neat room. The children saw no papers on the dresser or bedside table.

While they checked the wastebasket, Thiang searched the drawers. Then she opened the closet and looked through her brother's clothes, but found nothing.

"Maybe Sarad was in the dressing room when the call came," said Bert. "Perhaps he made a note of it there."

Thiang and the twins hurried downstairs again. Although the ballroom was dark, Thiang knocked at the door of the men's dressing room. No answer.

She opened the door and flicked a switch inside. Bright lights went on around a large mirror over a makeup table. Next to it on the wall was the telephone. The twins examined the room, but found no paper with an address.

"Maybe we ought to call the police," Nan said.

"Please, no! I don't want to do that!" Thiang exclaimed. "It might be bad publicity for the hotel. The manager has been so kind to all of us that I would hate to hurt his business."

"Besides," Bert added, "we are not certain that the thing Sarad went to see is the stolen cup. He might not have met the thieves. There may be some other reason why he's not back."

While Thiang and the older twins were talking, Flossie seated herself at the dressing table. She began playing with the paints that the dancers used to transform their faces into those of ancient Siamese characters. Now, as Nan turned, she saw her sister in the mirror.

"Flossie!" Nan cried.

The little girl's cheeks were bright with rouge and black lines curved around her eyes.

"You know better than to touch those things," Bert said sternly.

Flossie looked downcast. "I'm sorry, but the black pencils were such fun to draw with—" Her voice trailed off as she saw Nan's and Bert's disapproving faces.

Freddie giggled. "You look like a clown, Floss."

"It doesn't matter," said Thiang kindly. "The makeup comes off with cold cream."

Nan walked over to the dressing table. "All right, Flossie. Let's get you cleaned up."

She reached for a box of tissues which stood at the end of the mirror beside the telephone. Suddenly her eye was caught by the reflection of something black on the back of the box. She turned it over.

Written in eyebrow pencil were the words, *Rest-A-While Cottage—Lake Kewaga.*

"I've found it!" Nan exclaimed.

The others hastened to look. "Yes. That's Sarad's writing," said Thiang.

"Where is Lake Kewaga?" Freddie piped up. No one knew.

"Maybe it's one of the Footprint Lakes," said Bert. Then he said to Thiang, "If Sarad is not back by morning, I think you'd better call the police."

Just then there was a knock at the door, which was half open. A bellboy peered in. "Oh, there you are, miss. Telephone message for you," he said and handed Thiang a paper. "It came during the performance."

He hurried off as she thanked him and unfolded the note.

"It's from Sarad!" she exclaimed. "He says not to worry. He had to go to New York on important business and will be back tomorrow." She frowned. "It is not like him to go off this way."

Quickly Nan cleaned Flossie's face, and the twins said good night to the dancer.

"You are very helpful children," Thiang told them. "Thank you."

Both Mr. and Mrs. Bobbsey were in the lobby when the twins came out of the ballroom. Bert explained about Sarad's disappearance.

"Is Lake Kewaga far from here?" he asked.

"No," Mr. Bobbsey replied. "It is the smallest of the Footprint Lakes and is connected to this one by a canal."

"Then we can reach it easily if we have to," Bert thought.

Next morning the Bobbsey family went to church services in a nearby town. When they returned they found Thiang in the lobby. She said that Sarad had not returned.

"I'm worried," Nan confessed. "That telephone message last night might not have come from Sarad. It could have been a trick to keep you from going to the police right away."

"I've been thinking that, too," said Thiang.

"Maybe the bad men have Sarad," Flossie spoke up.

Bert nodded. "I'd like to check that cottage at Lake Kewaga."

"I will go too," said Thiang eagerly.

Mr. Bobbsey turned to her and said kindly, "I don't want to discourage you, but we can't be certain the address on the tissue box is the one given to Sarad by the man who called. It might have been written at some other time."

"But Dad, don't you think we ought to check?" Bert argued.

"Yes, I must go," insisted Thiang.

"Of course, we understand," said Mrs. Bobbsey. "If by any chance the thieves should be there, come back at once and get help."

The twins' mother invited Thiang to join the family at dinner in the hotel dining room. During the meal she persuaded the younger twins to stay home and play croquet with her and their father.

Afterwards the older children and the dancer hurried to the waterfront where Bert rented a canoe. Thiang sat in the middle while the twins paddled up to the canal and through it into Lake Kewaga.

"How are we going to find Rest-A-While Cottage?" Nan asked.

"It's a small lake," Bert replied. "Let's tie up at the first dock we see and walk around to the cottages."

A few minutes later Thiang pointed out a white boathouse and dock, and the children paddled over. They tied the canoe and made their way toward a run-down-looking cottage. "Well, what do you know!" Bert exclaimed. He pointed to a weather-beaten sign on the porch. "Rest-A-While Cottage!"

"It looks deserted," said Nan, eyeing the closed doors and windows.

"We'll find out." Bert went up and knocked on the door. There was no reply. He tried again. No answer. Finally he peered into one of the windows. "I don't see anybody."

"If my brother ever was here, he's gone now," said Thiang in a discouraged tone.

"Let's check the boathouse," Bert suggested.

They crossed the yard and peered through the open door into the gloomy interior.

"There's a hotel canoe here!" Bert said. "See! It has the words *Big Pine Hotel* on the side— like the one we have!"

"Then Sarad has been here! But where is he now?" his sister asked.

"Sh-h!" said Nan sharply, then whispered, "I think somebody is in here!"

The three stood silent. A soft rustling sound reached their ears.

Bert glanced up at the rafters of the boathouse. There was a narrow shelf on one side about two feet from the roof. In the middle of it crouched a grayish hump with two bright eyes.

Bert edged his way along the narrow walk which ran around the inside of the boathouse.

"It's a 'possum," he called back. Looking up, Bert saw a narrow hole in the roof. "He must have crawled in through that somehow and now I'll bet he can't get out."

"Could we help him?" Nan asked.

Looking around, Bert spotted an old sail crumpled in one corner. "If you girls will hold that out like a net, I'll try to nudge him off with a pole, and he can drop into it."

Nan and Thiang grasped corners of the sail and stretched it below the opossum. Bert took a long pole from another corner and began to prod the creature. At first it closed both eyes and lay still.

"It looks dead," said Thiang.

"He's playing 'possum," Bert told her and explained this was a trick these animals used when in danger.

Bert managed to get the end of the pole between the animal and the wall. He gave a gentle push.

"Catch him!" Bert exclaimed.

With a *plop* the opossum fell into the makeshift net. The girls carried it outside and put it on the ground.

Bert came beside them and the trio watched the animal from a distance. In a few minutes it stood up and ran off on its awkward-looking legs.

"Catch him!" Bert exclaimed

Nan giggled. "Old Mr. 'Possum thought he fooled us!"

"There is nothing more we can do here," said Bert. As he put the sail back in the boathouse, a sudden muffled thump came from the cabin.

"What was that?" Nan asked.

Again the noise.

"Something *is* in the house!" Thiang exclaimed.

Bert raced to the porch with the girls close behind him. The thumping grew louder. He tried the door and it opened.

Nan pointed to a closet at the side of the room. "The noise is in there," she said.

As the three ran toward the closet, the doorknob rattled and the key shook in the lock.

"Stand back!" Bert warned the girls. Then he turned the key and flung the door open.

CHAPTER X

A NOISY SHADOW

A SMALL, dark-haired man staggered out of the closet.

"Sarad!" cried Thiang. She embraced her brother and with the children's help led him to a chair.

"What happened?" she asked anxiously. Sarad tried to speak, but could not. Bert ran to the sink, found a glass and brought the man some water.

The dancer drank thirstily, then whispered, "Thank you. I called so long that I had no voice left."

"It was the thieves who locked you in that closet, wasn't it?" said Bert.

The small man looked up at the boy, his dark eyes puzzled. "Yes. How did you know?"

Thiang introduced the children. Then she explained their connection with the case.

Sarad told them that when he had arrived at

the cottage the morning before, he had found two men waiting.

"They showed me the elephant cup. I recognized it at once. They guessed I knew they had stolen it. The men asked for money. I told them I did not have any with me and would have to meet them a second time. Of course I meant to bring the police. But they saw that I suspected them."

"So they were afraid to let you go," said Nan.

"How terrible for you!" Thiang exclaimed.

"I slept part of the time—I was worn out with yelling and pounding," Sarad told her.

"I guess that's why you didn't hear us knock on the door," remarked Bert.

"Do you know where the two men went from here?" Nan asked anxiously. "Did they say anything about the elephant?"

The dancer nodded. "After they locked me in the closet, I heard them talking. They said how hard it had been to get the cup away from the elephant. The little man wants to get rid of the animal, but the tall one is determined to sell her to a carnival or a circus."

"Do you know where she is?" Bert asked.

"In an old factory somewhere," was the reply. "I heard the little man say they couldn't hold her there much longer because she was making too much noise."

"That's a wonderful lead!" Bert said. "Did you learn anything else?"

"No," the dancer replied, "except that the tall man's name is Crow and the short one is called Lester."

Thiang told her brother about the false message.

He nodded. "Lester made the call."

Bert helped Sarad to his canoe in the boathouse, then paddled him back to the hotel. Thiang and Nan followed in the other craft.

When Mr. Bobbsey heard the story, he telephoned the Lakeport police. Then he reported to his family, who were waiting in the lobby with the dancers.

"Sarad and Thiang are to tell their story to the local police right away," he said. "We Bobbseys are to go at once to headquarters in Lakeport."

"Why?" asked Bert.

"Chief Smith says he would like to have you children help the police." Mrs. Bobbsey looked surprised and her husband said, "He promises there is no danger."

"What are we to do, Dad?" asked Nan.

"The chief will tell us when we get there," said Mr. Bobbsey.

"You are very brave children," Sarad told the twins. "Many thanks for your help." Thiang also thanked them and wished them luck.

Without delay the family packed and left. It was dark by the time Mr. Bobbsey drew up in front of Lakeport police headquarters. Chief

Smith was waiting for them in his office. Quickly he told them that a squad of his men was going to investigate several deserted factories on the outskirts of town.

"We hope to take the thieves by surprise. But the problem is the elephant. I am afraid she will get wind of the officers and raise a fuss. This would alert the two men and spoil the plan.

"But Mr. Burns told me she's not afraid of you children," he went on. "You could sneak up without exciting her, report to us and if the men are there, we can rush the place."

"It's a keen plan!" Bert exclaimed.

"You would be in touch with three officers in the car by walkie-talkie. A fourth man can be a few yards behind you. Each child may have a police whistle. We would like all of you on the job, because there is safety in numbers." He turned to Mr. and Mrs. Bobbsey. "How about it?"

The children's parents exchanged looks. "All right," said Mr. Bobbsey. "But they must be cautious and obey orders."

The twins promised and Bert carefully took the walkie-talkie the chief handed him. Then the man gave each of them a police whistle on a cord which they put around their necks.

"The squad car's waiting," he said. "Good luck!"

Minutes later they drove off. Officer Lane was

behind the wheel. Beside him was Brown, who introduced the other policemen as Carson and Denver.

As they rode through the downtown streets, Lane gave them their instructions. Officer Carson made sure all of them knew how to use the walkie-talkie.

"It won't be long now," said Denver as the lights of the town were left behind.

The car headed down the dark river road. Soon their driver pulled off and parked behind a screen of bushes.

Across a field of high weeds the children could see a low building at the water's edge. Some distance upstream stood another.

"Start with this factory," said Officer Lane. "If you have no luck here, scout around that one. Keep us alerted and we'll follow along in the car. Denver is your shadow. He'll be about five yards behind you in case of trouble. He has a walkie-talkie, too. Okay?"

"Okay," Bert replied.

When the children got out of the car, Brown gave the older twins flashlights. "Don't use these unless you have to," he warned. "We don't want anyone to see you."

The children started off single file. Except for the soft *swish* of the weeds, all was quiet. Once Nan looked back for Officer Denver, but there was no sign of him.

Bert guessed what she was thinking and plucked her sleeve. "Don't worry," he whispered. "He's there. He keeps down."

As the children drew closer to the factory, they saw that the windows were black holes with the glass broken out. The front door hung on one hinge. Over it they could make out a sign which said DIX FLAG COMPANY.

The twins slipped around the building, looking for a light inside. The one-story structure was dark. They did not see a car or truck.

They stopped at the back of the building and listened. All they could hear was the lapping of the river against the nearby bank.

"We'd better check inside," said Bert.

When they reached the front again, he stepped cautiously through the door. The others followed.

"Boy, it sure is dark," thought Freddie and clutched his whistle.

Soon the twins could see they were in a short corridor. On one side was a half-open door marked "Office." Straight ahead was an archway which they guessed led to a main room. Bert peered into the office, then stepped toward the arch. A board squeaked loudly under his foot. The twins froze and strained their ears. *Were the thieves here? Had they heard the noise?* The building was silent.

Flossie turned and peered into the office. She saw a big roundish shape in one corner.

"Like an elephant!" she thought and turned back to tell the others. They had disappeared. All was silent. Flossie's knees began to shake.

"Have the bad men caught them?" she wondered. For a few minutes she stood rooted, afraid to move.

Suddenly there was a rustle from the office. In terror Flossie bolted through the arch.

"Ow!" she cried as a stick hit her shin. She stumbled and fell. The next moment a heavy cloth dropped over her.

"Help!" Flossie shrieked. "Bert! Nan!" The little girl struggled wildly inside the folds. Suddenly the material was pulled away.

"Flossie!" came Nan's voice. Bert and Freddie helped the little girl to her feet.

"Something got me!" Flossie exclaimed.

As Nan snapped on her light, the boys picked up a huge old banner with the words on it, "Foster High School Band."

Freddie explained that the flag probably had been propped up by the door. "You tripped and it fell on you."

Nan put an arm around her little sister. "You're all right now, Floss. There's nobody here. We've checked. See? The factory is just this one big room."

Nan flashed her light around at rows of abandoned sewing machines and boxes stacked against the wall.

Just then a flashlight appeared in the doorway. "Everything all right?" asked a low voice. "I thought I heard a noise."

"We're okay, officer," said Bert. "We'll be right out. This place is empty."

"Check," said the detective and melted into the darkness.

"It's a good thing that flag muffled your screams," Bert said to his little sister, "or the whole squad of police would be here by now."

"I'm sorry," said Flossie. Suddenly she remembered her discovery. "I think I saw Baby May!" Taking Bert's hand, she led the way to the office. "Look!" she whispered excitedly. "In the corner!"

The older twins beamed their lights into the room. There was an old rolltop desk!

"Oh," said Flossie, crestfallen. "But I know I heard something in there."

"Probably a mouse," said Nan. "We saw some."

After she and Bert switched off their lights, the children left the building and walked along the riverbank toward the next factory. It was a black hulk, so old it leaned sideways. The windows were boarded up. Here and there around the wooden walls grew wild clumps of brush.

Avoiding these, the twins walked to the front. Amid the high grass they crossed a concrete drive, which came from River Road. It ended at a wooden ramp which led up to ramshackle double doors.

"Look! In the corner!"

The twins rounded the building. Suddenly they heard crackling in the bushes and ducked into the weeds. Silence. Cautiously the children moved on. Again the crackling of a twig!

Freddie took Nan's hand. "Somebody's following us," he whispered.

Nan put her lips close to his ear and said, "Probably Officer Denver." But she wondered why such a skillful tracker did not avoid the bushes.

Bert wondered, too. "Maybe it's a rabbit," he told himself, hoping that it was.

At his signal the children crept around to the back of the old factory. There was no car or truck which might have belonged to the thieves.

"Maybe this is the wrong factory, too," Bert thought.

Nan tapped him on the shoulder. She pointed to a dim light coming through a knothole. The twins hurried over and Nan put her eye to the hole. Tethered to a large piece of machinery was Baby May!

The next instant the light went out!

CHAPTER XI

THE CHASE

NAN stepped back from the knothole. "Baby May is in there," she whispered. "One of the men must be with her."

"Did you see him?" Bert asked eagerly.

"No, but someone turned the light off."

"Maybe he heard us and he's coming out!" said Freddie.

"The other man must have gone somewhere with their car or truck," Bert reasoned.

The twins moved away from the building. Quickly Bert reported to the police on his walkie-talkie.

A low, squawky voice replied and gave the twins orders. The girls and Freddie were to hide near the front door. When the capture was over, the police would pick them up. Bert was to stay with Officer Denver.

As Nan slipped away with the young twins, the policeman appeared. At his request Bert showed him the knothole. The officer put his ear to it, trying to hear what was going on in the dark building. Meanwhile the others crept behind a clump of bushes beside the ramp.

"I'm so 'cited, I'm shivering," Flossie whispered.

"Shh! Listen!" said Nan. The muffled sound of a man's voice came from inside the factory.

Suddenly the elephant trumpeted. Then they heard the man give several loud grunts. More trumpeting and grunting followed.

The children scrambled onto the ramp and tried to see through a crack between the doors. It was too dark.

"What's going on?" Freddie whispered anxiously.

"I don't know, but I wish the police would hurry," said Nan as the elephant sounded off again.

"Don't worry," Flossie said. "Baby May is safe. The man can't take her away. We didn't see any car or truck."

Freddie chuckled. "He's caught too!"

Suddenly there was the roar of a motor, then the loud honking of an automobile horn. The children could not believe their ears!

"It's inside!" Freddie exclaimed. "Coming this way!"

"Jump!" cried Nan.

As the three children leaped off the ramp, the rickety doors burst apart and a black station

"Jump!" cried Nan

wagon shot out of the building, with the horn blaring.

Blowing on their whistles, the girls and Freddie crashed out of the bushes. Nan flashed her light at the car just in time to see the elephant standing in the back and reaching over the front seat to blow the horn with her trunk! Through the open window they could hear the tall driver shouting angrily while the little man struggled to make the elephant stop.

"Catch them!" shouted Bert as he raced up with Officer Denver.

"They're getting away with Baby May!" cried Freddie, as they all ran after the fleeing car.

Suddenly a siren wailed and a pair of headlights swept into the drive, speeding head-on toward the station wagon!

"They'll hit!" Nan screamed.

Brakes squealing, the police car stopped. Inches away, the station wagon swerved through the weeds, then shot back onto the concrete and roared away.

The door of the police car was thrown open. "Hurry, children!" shouted Officer Lane.

The children dashed over with Denver and piled into the car. It made a bumpy U-turn through the weeds, jolted onto the drive and sped after the station wagon, siren squealing. The pursuers could see taillights ahead and hear the horn honking.

Bert grinned. "Keep it up, Baby May!" he exclaimed.

While Officer Brown radioed the alarm to patrol cars, Freddie bounced up and down on the seat in excitement. "They'll never get away now! Nobody can miss that car with the horn blowing!"

"Hurry! Hurry!" cried Flossie.

The station wagon swerved onto a side road which led toward the river.

"They're heading for the drawbridge!" Bert exclaimed.

Nan pointed across the open field to some lights on the water. "A boat's coming! The bridge will go up any minute now. They'll have to stop!"

The pursuers could see the station wagon racing toward the span and the wooden gate starting down.

"We've got 'em!" Bert said happily. "They'll never make it across!"

But the next instant the thieves' car spurted ahead and shot under the lowering bar. The station wagon sped over the bridge.

"They're racing to get under that gate at the other end," said Officer Brown, "but they'll never make it."

A moment later both barricades were down. "They have to stop now," said Nan.

But the station wagon went faster. *Crack!* The sound of splintering wood carried clearly as the big car smashed straight through the gate.

"Oh no!" chorused the twins in dismay and the men looked grim. By the time their car reached the bridge, the fleeing station wagon had disappeared down a street across the river. The two halves of the span were slowly rising.

While Officer Brown reported the escape over his radio, the twins watched anxiously for the bridge to close. After ten minutes, which seemed like an hour, the two sides came down again. The gates went up and the police car shot ahead.

The attendant on the other side waved wildly at them. Officer Brown shouted that more police would be along soon.

As they drove into the small business district beyond the shattered gate, the police party saw a crowd standing on a corner, talking excitedly.

Officer Lane slowed down and Bert leaned out of the window. "Did you see a black station—" he began.

"That way!" chorused the bystanders, pointing down the main street.

"Thanks!" called Bert as the car leaped forward. Confused shouts followed and a man cried, "An elephant was driving!"

Farther on, Officer Lane stopped again to ask two men if they had seen the station wagon.

"Straight ahead, up the hill!" one replied.

The pursuers drove on. At the top of the hill, they looked out over a dark expanse of rolling farmland. The road lay over it like a light ribbon.

"I don't see any taillights," said Bert.

"Or hear a horn," added Freddie.

"They're probably over a hill," Officer Lane remarked. He grinned. "Maybe Lester got the elephant to stop the racket."

The children watched anxiously, but no red lights appeared.

"That's funny. I didn't think they were that far ahead of us," said Nan.

Officer Brown shook his head. "Neither did I, but they were pushing that black buggy pretty fast."

"It might have turned off some place," Bert suggested.

The twins watched carefully from the windows for side roads and drives. For a mile they saw nothing but large trees on either hand. Then the car rattled over a narrow wooden bridge. Bert and Nan looked down into a steep gully.

"Wait!" Nan cried. "See that moving flashlight down there beside the water."

"I see it!" said Bert excitedly.

Officer Lane pulled onto the shoulder of the road.

"Okay," he said, swinging out of the car. "You two show us exactly where you spotted the light. Denver, come with me. Brown and Carson stay here and keep the motor running. If anyone tries to sneak out of that gully, nab him!" He turned to Freddie and Flossie. "In that case, you blow your whistles."

Bert and Nan left their flashlights and walkie-talkie in case the young twins should need them. They got out of the car and led the three men up the road. Reaching the bridge, they spotted the flashlight moving away from them, some distance up the gully.

"Wait here while we investigate," Officer Lane said softly to Bert and Nan.

The two men hurried away along the water. The children moved off the road and stood on the pebbly ground next to the bridge.

They waited tensely, watching the flashlight move along the creek. Neither twin spoke nor moved.

They saw the officers disappear into the ravine. Minutes went by. The light continued moving away. There was no sound. *What had happened to the policemen?*

Nan shifted uneasily and a small pebble rattled down the steep slope. She looked into the gully and saw only the gleam of the water.

Suddenly from the darkness below came a muffled voice. "Try it again!"

A man replied harshly, "It's no use, I tell you!"

Two men were under the bridge! As the twins strained forward to hear more, Bert's feet slipped and the gravel began to roll. With a cry, he lost his balance and slid into the gully!

CHAPTER XII

THE TATTOOED COOK

A SHOWER of pebbles rattled down as Bert plunged along the slope. He landed in the shallow water of the creek. Startled exclamations came from under the bridge and someone hauled him to his feet. He could hear Nan on the brink of the gully blowing her police whistle.

"What's that? Who are you?" came the harsh voice, and a light was flashed in the boy's face.

The man who was holding Bert let him go. "It's just some kid," he said.

Bert could see that both men were short and stocky. The first speaker was bald. The other had a gray mustache. A small car stood under the bridge.

"Where are the police?" the bald man asked. "What's going on?"

"We were looking for some men, but you're the wrong ones," Bert explained breathlessly.

Just then there were shouts and the three policemen came splashing up with a fourth officer.

"I told you to stay on the bank, Bert," said Officer Lane sternly.

"He fell," said the bald man. "What's all this about anyway?"

"We'll ask the questions," said Officer Carson coolly. "How did this car get here?"

The policemen's flashlights were trained on the two men and Bert saw that they wore overalls and had weather-beaten faces.

"It was an accident," said the bald man. "We were headed for Stockton. The road crossed this creek about a mile from here. There's a sharp turn just before the bridge. We missed it and landed in the gully."

The fellow with the mustache spoke up. "Lucky we landed right side up. The creek is shallow so we decided to ride in it until we could drive out. But when we got this far the car stalled."

The officers checked the men's identification and promised them they would send help. Then Bert and the policemen climbed up the steep slope to Nan.

"I heard it all," she said. "Did you get hurt?"

"Just got my feet and legs wet," Bert replied.

When the twins reached the car they reported what had happened.

"We heard the whistle," Officer Brown said, "and I got out, expecting to see the elephant-nappers running away."

Flossie sighed and said, "Poor Baby May. We didn't save her after all."

"Don't worry. The alarm has gone out over all the neighboring states," said Officer Brown. He grinned. "Two men and an elephant in a station wagon can't get very far away. Somebody's sure to pick them up."

Next morning, however, there was no news of the strange trio.

"I hope we have better luck finding Tippy," said Freddie, as he buttered his toast.

Nan nodded. "If we don't locate Tippy by midnight day after tomorrow, she won't get the prize."

"At least we have a lead on Tippy's case," said Bert. "Mother, would you drive us to Fun Lake this afternoon? Maybe the excursion boat there is the *Sea Sprite*."

"Yes. I'll pick you up after school, so we don't waste any time," she replied. "Fun Lake's two hours away."

When they reached the parking lot later that afternoon the children could see a roller coaster and other rides of the amusement park. To one side was a trailer camp.

"Maybe Tippy's sister lives in one of those trailers," said Nan. "Let's inquire."

Leaving Mrs. Bobbsey in the car, the twins

hurried into the camp. Some distance away they saw a gray-haired man carrying a folding chair out of a blue trailer. They walked over to him.

"Excuse me, but we're looking for somebody," said Nan. She introduced herself and the others. Bert took the photograph from his wallet and the man looked at it.

"Sorry I can't help you," he said. "This is the first year I've camped here. You'd better ask somebody else."

The twins looked around at the circle of trailers. The metal shutters on most of them were closed and no one was in sight.

"I don't think there's anybody else to ask," Freddie spoke up.

"It's pretty early in the season for most folks," the man replied, "but there is another couple here." He pointed to a silver-colored trailer. "It looks as if they've gone out. Why don't you come back later?"

The children thanked the camper and returned to their mother.

Bert told her what they had found out, then said, "Let's ask some of the people who work at the amusement park if they know Tippy's sister. We can check on that excursion boat, too."

Mrs. Bobbsey agreed. She led the way to the admission booth and bought five tickets. As the twins went through the gate, she said, "You go ahead. I'll follow after I buy a program."

The children started down a midway with booths on either side.

"Let's try the shooting gallery," said Bert. He walked over to a counter lined with rifles. Rows of white metal ducks moved along the back wall.

An attendant beamed at them. "How about it, friends? Try your luck! Shoot a duck!"

"Not just now," said Nan politely. "We want to ask you something."

Bert showed him the picture of Tippy and Margery in front of the *Sea Sprite*. "Do you know either of these two ladies?"

For a moment the man looked at the twins, puzzled, then he glanced at the picture. "No, never saw them before."

"How about the boat?" Bert asked. At that moment the attendant's eyes rested on two boys who had come up to the counter. "The excursion boat's at the lake, sonny," he said quickly and walked over to his new customers.

Bert shrugged and put the picture away. "Come on, let's try somewhere else."

As the twins moved down the street, the odor of popcorn came to them. At a stand just ahead they could see the white kernels popping around inside a clear container. Next to it in a glass case was a big mound of the golden buttery corn.

"I'm hungry," announced Freddie. The others said they were, too.

"We'll get one box," said Nan. "That way we won't spoil our supper."

She hurried to the counter and bought a carton. Munching popcorn, the children trotted gaily along, with Mrs. Bobbsey strolling behind. Freddie ran back to offer her some popcorn.

As he returned to the others, Nan suddenly exclaimed, "Look what I see!" She pointed to a large sign across the front of a nearby booth: MRS. MARTIN'S DO-NUTS.

"Maybe this Mrs. Martin is a relative of Tippy and her sister," Nan said.

"And can tell us where Margery lives," Flossie added.

The twins hurried up to the counter, where a stout boy in a white apron stood waiting to serve them.

"May we see Mrs. Martin, please?" Bert asked.

The boy looked at them oddly. "Mrs. Martin?" he asked.

"Yes. Is she here?" Nan asked.

The boy grinned. "Sure. I'll call her." He went through curtains at the back of the booth and in a few moments returned, smiling more widely than ever.

Out came a big muscular man wiping his hands on a white apron. His shirt sleeves were rolled up, and on each arm he had a blue anchor tattoo. With a twinkle in his eye, he said:

"I'm Mrs. Martin," he said

"I'm Mrs. Martin. What can I do for you?"

As the twins looked surprised, he laughed and explained that for some years he had been a cook in the navy. When he got out, he had decided to go into the doughnut business.

"I used my mother's recipe, so I decided to name the doughnuts after her."

The twins giggled. Bert told the man what they were doing and asked if he were a relative of Tippy's. He said, "No." Then Bert showed him the photograph. The man had never seen either of the two women.

Just then Mrs. Bobbsey strolled up. "The doughnuts smell yummy," Flossie said. "May we have some, Mommy?"

"They do look good," Mrs. Bobbsey agreed. "We'll get a dozen. Then we can take some home for Daddy."

When the fragrant, sugared doughnuts were in the bag, the cook excused himself. Bert asked the assistant the name of the excursion boat.

The stout boy looked vague. "*Sea* something," he replied.

Bert thanked him and said to the others, "Let's go over to the waterfront and look at that boat."

"Yes, hurry," said Nan. "It sounds as if this is the right lake!"

"When are we going to eat the doughnuts?" Freddie put in.

"After supper," replied his mother firmly.

The children hurried past a few more booths, then turned down a walk which led to the tree-lined shore. Straight ahead was a white dock with a sign over it: EXCURSION BOAT.

"Here it comes!" cried Freddie excitedly. Chugging toward the dock was a big launch with a striped canopy over the top.

"Is it the *Sea Sprite?*" Nan asked quickly.

The name was still invisible. The children ran toward the dock, and a moment later the words on the bow came into sight. Freddie opened his mouth to shout with joy. Then he saw his mistake.

"The Sea Nymph!" Nan exclaimed. The twins' faces fell.

"Well, that's that!" Bert said.

The four walked over to their mother, who had seen the boat and seated herself on a bench under a tree. "Too bad, children," she said.

"I guess it's no use hanging around here any longer," Bert remarked.

Freddie and Flossie looked longingly at a small dock some distance away. In front of it a section of the lake had been roped off where small, brightly colored boats moved back and forth.

"May we ride one of those little pedal boats, Mother, please?" Flossie asked.

"Yes, if you wish. I'll wait for you here."

"Let's go with them, Bert," said Nan.

The children walked over to the admission booth and bought four tickets.

"I want to pedal and steer," said Freddie.

"So do I," said his twin.

A dock attendant helped Flossie and Bert into one boat and Nan and Freddie into another. A moment later they were skimming over the water.

Freddie waved at his twin and Bert, who were making a wide turn. "Better keep both hands on the wheel," said Nan.

"Don't worry, it's not crowded," her brother replied. He glanced around at the half dozen boats which were moving about the enclosure.

As he did, his eye caught sight of two figures on the shore. The boy gasped and pointed.

"Freddie! Watch out!" Nan cried.

Straight ahead was a green boat! The next moment came the collision!

Freddie had hit it!

CHAPTER XIII

A LAKE MONSTER

THE two boats rocked wildly. The boy in the green one glared at Freddie. "Why don't you watch where you're going?" he demanded.

"I'm sorry," said Freddie. "Are you hurt?"

"No," the boy replied. "So long, cowboy!" He pedaled off.

"I told you to keep your hands on the wheel," said Nan. "What were you pointing at?"

"I saw Lester on the shore."

Nan looked. "I don't see him. Are you sure, Freddie?"

"Yes. He had on his checkered jacket."

"Head for the dock! Maybe we can catch him!" said Nan quickly. She called to Bert and Flossie to bring in their boat. In a few minutes the four children were ashore and Nan explained what had happened. As they hurried toward their mother, the twins looked around but did not see Lester or his pal.

When Mrs. Bobbsey heard the news, she stood

up quickly. "We must inform the park police at once!"

Nan saw an officer nearby and brought him over. After Bert described Crow and Lester, the officer went off to start a search.

"We ought to look, too," said Nan.

Bert suggested that his mother and the young twins start at one end of the amusement area while he and Nan began at the other.

"The park is narrow and runs along the lake," Nan said, "so I think we have a good chance to find the men—if they're still here."

"We'll walk toward each other, watching all the time," Bert said. "If we spot the men, one of us can run for a policeman."

Mrs. Bobbsey agreed. "We'll meet in the center plaza," she added. The two teams separated.

The older twins trotted along the lake shore, hunting for the thieves. Reaching the low back fence of the park, they cut onto a path which led to the amusement section between the rows of noisy, colorful rides.

"I can't figure out," said Bert, "what those fellows are doing in an amusement park." Nan was puzzled, too.

As they passed the Haunted House, the twins heard shrieks. They glanced up at the gallery and saw several people disappearing through a swinging door.

"Bert!" Nan exclaimed. "I saw a checkered jacket!"

"Was it Lester?" her brother asked.

"I don't know. I just caught a glimpse."

The children stationed themselves outside and watched the laughing people come out of a cobwebby hole.

Suddenly a strange young man appeared in a checkered jacket just like the one the thief wore.

Bert and Nan sighed and walked on.

Together they scanned passing faces and stopped to check on people in front of booths.

"It's like looking for a needle in a haystack," Nan remarked.

Both children were hot and discouraged. Bert and Nan saw Mrs. Bobbsey and the young twins. They were standing in front of a circular building with a big EATS sign on the roof.

"Did you see the thief?" Bert asked eagerly.

"No, just two false alarms. We might as well have something to eat. I told Dinah not to expect us."

Inside the restaurant, the Bobbseys looked for Crow and Lester but did not see them.

Later when the family came out of the restaurant, the lights in the park had been turned on. The place was more crowded now and music filled the air.

As the children munched doughnuts, Flossie looked up at the make-believe airplanes whizzing in a circle, each on a long cable. "I wish we could stay and go on the rides," she said.

"Oh yes, please," Freddie begged. "We haven't any homework."

"Bert and I are doing extra book reports," said Nan, "so we don't have any either."

"All right then," said Mrs. Bobbsey. It was agreed that the older twins would meet the others beside the merry-go-round at nine o'clock.

Bert and Nan promised, and started off by themselves. "Let's take a ride on the *Sea Nymph,*" Nan suggested.

Bert bought two tickets at the dock and the pair joined the small crowd on the launch. The captain, a stocky man with a red face, wore a white coat and a cap with gold braid on it.

"All aboard!" he cried.

He pulled a rope and a bell clanged twice. A moment later the boat chugged out onto the darkening lake. The lights of the park twinkled along the shore.

"Now, folks," boomed the captain, "I have to warn you that there is a monster in this lake. Maybe we'll see him, maybe we won't!"

The people laughed and a few of them clapped.

Suddenly Nan grabbed her brother's arm and pointed out over the water. A motorboat with two men in it was speeding toward the far end of the lake. One man was tall, the other short.

"It could be Lester and Crow!" Bert said.

At that moment the water heaved up in front of the launch. A huge black rubbery creature that looked like a sea serpent rose from the depths.

"It's the monster!" Nan exclaimed.

The passengers screamed and laughed as the monster's electric eyes winked and the mouth spouted water. On the side was a glowing sign which said *Enjoy Fun Lake*. The creature bobbed up and down for a few moments, then sank under the waves.

When Bert and Nan could see ahead once more, the motorboat with the two suspects in it had vanished. "It was going toward the woods at the far end of the lake," said Bert. "Maybe the captain will let us off there."

The children hurried to ask him. The stocky man shook his head. "Sorry. That's against the rules."

After what seemed a long time the boat completed its round trip and returned to the dock.

As Nan hurried ashore she said to her brother, "What do you think we ought to do?"

Bert replied, "I'd say tell the park police, but we're not absolutely sure that the men were Crow and Lester."

"That's right," Nan remarked. "After all, they had their backs to us and the light was not very good."

"Let's walk up to the end of the lake," Bert suggested, "and try to find them. If they are the thieves, we can run back and get the police."

The twins hastened along the shore. They

"It's the monster!" Nan exclaimed

climbed over the back fence. Trotting on, they
kept between the water's edge and the dark
woods. After a while the gay music and the
screams from the roller coaster grew faint. Near
the end of the lake, they heard voices. Cautiously the twins slipped into the woods and
moved toward the sounds.

Suddenly a bright flame showed through the
trees. A campfire! Drawing closer, Bert and
Nan saw three men seated around a stone barbecue pit. Two of the men were Crow and Lester!
The third was a fat man in a shiny brown suit.
His pasty face looked anxious as he glanced toward the woods where the twins were hidden.

"I thought I heard something," the man said
hoarsely.

"So what?" Lester asked. He was holding a
hot dog sandwich in one hand. With the other he
brushed crumbs off his checkered coat. "If anybody comes along, we're just three fellows having a picnic. We can't be arrested for that, can
we?"

"No, but they could put me in jail for buying
a stolen elephant," the fat man said.

Crow pointed his hot dog at him. "There's no
danger, I'm telling you! And the animal's a
great bargain, Mr. Froom! Besides," he added,
"all your carnivals are way out West. Who's
going to connect any of your animals with the
one that was stolen here?"

Mr. Froom shook his head. "I don't know,"

he said slowly. "I came East to buy animals, but I don't want to risk buying stolen property."

"Risk!" exclaimed Crow, looking astonished. "Why, it's easy as pie! You bring your truck to the meeting place and pay us the money. We load the elephant and away you go!"

"I want to think it over," said the fat man. "I'm staying with a friend. I'll give you his phone number and—"

"Tonight will be your last chance," said Crow quickly. "We have another customer."

Mr. Froom rubbed his hands together nervously. Finally he said, "All right. Where shall I come?"

The thieves smiled, and Crow reached into his pocket. He pulled out a piece of white paper and handed it to the carnival owner. "Here is a map I drew. The time is written on it, too."

Mr. Froom studied the paper carefully for a few minutes.

"Take it with you," said Crow.

"No, no!" Froom said quickly. "I don't want any evidence on me."

"It's all set!" exclaimed Crow. "We'll see you tomorrow afternoon."

"I'm warning you, though," said the fat man, "if anybody else finds out about this, the sale's off."

He started to walk away. At that instant Froom noticed that he still had the paper in his hand. He crumpled the sheet, and it dropped to the ground. Then he hurried through the woods toward the park.

As soon as he was out of sight, Crow slapped his partner on the shoulder. "We've sold the elephant! I told you it was a good idea to visit that animal dealer in New York. We landed a customer there, just like I said we would!"

"You're smart, all right, Crow," said Lester, "but I still don't see why we had to come way out here to close the deal."

The tall man looked disgusted. "If I've told you once I've told you a thousand times, we *must be careful!* Besides, Froom is scared. We had to have the meeting some place where he'd feel safe." Crow glanced at his partner's doubtful face. "Cheer up, it's all settled!"

Lester shook his head. "Not until we have his money, and he has our elephant." Then he said pleadingly, "Let's take the cup and get out of this area! It's getting too hot around here, Crow! The police are combing the countryside for us."

"I know some collectors in this neighborhood," said Crow sharply, "and we're not moving until I make contact with them." He stood up and started to kick out the fire. Lester helped him gloomily.

"Another thing," the short man burst out, "those Bobbsey twins are looking for us!" Then he added, "I thought I spied them in those little pedal boats."

Crow's face hardened. "If I catch those kids hanging around here, they'll be sorry."

Lester nodded. "Wouldn't I like to get my hands on those nosey kids!"

The two men turned and began walking straight toward the trees where Bert and Nan were hidden!

CHAPTER XIV

THE ANIMAL PRISONER

"THEY'LL find us!" Nan thought as the thieves drew closer to their hiding place.

The twins were just about to break cover and run through the woods, when the tall man stopped. "Wait! Let's not leave that map lying around," he said.

As Crow and Lester turned back to search for the paper, the children retreated a little distance. They could still hear and see the men.

"Why bother looking for it?" Lester grumbled. "There's nobody here to find it but the squirrels."

"Here it is!" said Crow. He carried the map to the barbecue pit and dropped it onto the embers. "Now let's get out of here." The men plunged into the woods.

As soon as they had passed, the twins ran quietly to the barbecue pit. They were just in time to see the map curl into ashes.

"Oh no!" Nan wailed softly. A moment later

they heard the roar of a motorboat and guessed that the men had hidden it in a cove nearby.

"We must report to the police at once," said Bert.

The children put the fire out completely, then hurried through the woods toward the amusement park. Soon they saw the pink glow in the sky from the colored lights and heard the gay music.

When they reached the merry-go-round, they found the young twins waiting with balloons. Mrs. Bobbsey stood beside them. Breathlessly Nan told their adventure, while Bert hurried to the office of the park police.

In a little while he returned. "The captain there thinks Froom will be hard to trace because he's not staying in a motel or a hotel."

The twins and their mother were worried.

"If the police don't locate those thieves by tomorrow," said Nan, "we may never see Baby May again."

Bert spoke up gloomily, "And if we don't find Tippy by midnight tomorrow, she'll lose her prize!"

"It looks as if we're at a dead end in both cases," Nan said sadly.

Nothing changed until the next day at noon. The telephone rang and the twins' mother answered. The children, who had just come home from school for luncheon, heard her mention the police chief's name.

When she finished talking, Mrs. Bobbsey smiled and said, "Bert, Chief Smith has had a tip that Baby May is on a houseboat up the river near Milford. He wants you to go there with three policemen this afternoon and be advance scout—the way you were at the factory."

"That's great!" exclaimed Bert.

Freddie spoke up. "You mean he doesn't have to go back to school?"

"That's right," Mrs. Bobbsey replied. She explained that the chief of police had called the principal. "Mr. Tetlow had said that Bert might be excused if I gave permission."

Flossie's eyes sparkled. "Oh, I hope you find Baby May!" she exclaimed. "Maybe she'll be home safe by suppertime!"

But Nan was not so sure. As she walked back to school with the young twins, she kept thinking of the elephant-nappers. The black station wagon had vanished very quickly after reaching the farmland.

"I can't help feeling that the thieves are hiding Baby May somewhere across the river," Nan said.

"Then why don't we search there after school?" Freddie asked.

"That's what I was thinking, too. We can take our bikes," said Nan.

Flossie spoke up cheerfully. "But if Bert finds Baby May on a houseboat, we won't have to go."

When the three returned home after school, there had been no word from their brother. Nan told her mother the plan.

"Go ahead," said Mrs. Bobbsey, "but the police must have searched that area pretty carefully by now."

Nan invited Nellie, and half an hour later the four children were pedaling across the drawbridge. Soon they were pumping up the hill which led to the farmland. At the top they paused, breathless, and looked out over the rolling hills. Some were planted with grain, others were dotted with grazing cows.

Nellie's eyes grew big. "You mean we have to search all of this?"

"As much as we can," said Nan firmly. "I think we ought to ask about Baby May at every farmhouse."

"And look in every deserted barn and shed," added Freddie. "Come on!"

The children coasted down the long hill with the wind whipping through their hair. When they reached the bottom, the four of them pedaled along briskly. They crossed the little wooden bridge and after a while saw a white farmhouse ahead.

Outside, a tall, thin woman was adding brightly colored shirts to a line of wash. She was holding several clothespins in her mouth.

The children left their bicycles at the side of the road and walked over to her. "Excuse me," said Nan, "but could you tell us if there are any deserted barns around here?"

The woman took the clothespins out of her mouth. "Why do you want to know?" she asked.

"We're looking for a missing elephant—the one that was stolen from the zoo," said Nan.

"Yes, I heard about that," the woman said. "I only know two old barns. One belongs to the Miller family, the other to the Wests. But the police searched both of those." She smiled. "They examined all the property along this road—barns, garages, tool sheds, everything!"

The children looked disappointed. "Thanks anyway," Nan said to the woman, and the four went back to their bicycles.

"It doesn't seem," said Nellie, "as if there's much use going on if the police have already searched everywhere."

"But maybe they missed a place," Nan replied hopefully. "I think we ought to keep looking."

"If somebody doesn't find Baby May today, she may be gone forever," said Flossie anxiously.

"Not if we keep looking," Freddie answered.

The children pedaled on, with the road winding between green fields. As they rounded a bend in the road, they saw a huge willow tree in a meadow. Its long leafy branches hung nearly to the ground and swung lightly in the wind.

As they rode past, Flossie turned to look at the tree. Her eyes grew wide in surprise.

"Nan!" she called. "Wait!"

The older girls stopped and Flossie drew up beside them with Freddie close behind her.

"What's the matter, Floss?" Nan asked.

"There's a car under that tree!" said the little girl. "I saw the wheels and part of the front when the wind blew the branches. Isn't that a funny place to put a car?"

The children looked back at the willow tree. "It must be thirty feet from the road," said Nellie. "That's no place to park."

"Maybe somebody's trying to hide it," said Freddie.

"Yes," his big sister agreed. "We'd better have a look."

The searchers wheeled their bicycles off the road and laid them at the edge of the pasture. Then they walked toward the large willow tree.

"Hey!" exclaimed Freddie. "What if the bad men are in the car?"

"Shh!" said Nan and Nellie.

The children crept forward and paused. Nan reached over, took a handful of the green branches and moved them aside.

Flossie gave a loud gasp. Hitched behind a green station wagon was a large two-wheeled crate. It was made of heavy boards about four inches apart, bound together with iron.

Nan's heart began to pound with excitement. Maybe Baby May was in the crate! She and

Nellie looked around uneasily. Where were the men? No one was in sight.

Flossie and Freddie had hurried straight to the crate. "Baby May," Flossie called softly, "are you in there?"

A rustle sounded inside. Then from between the boards a small gray trunk swung out!

"How can we ever get Baby May out of her prison?" Freddie cried out.

At once they began to talk to the elephant, cooed at her and patted her trunk.

Shrill trumpeting came from the animal. "She knows us!" said Flossie happily. "Oh, Baby May honey, are you hungry?"

Nellie and Nan searched their pockets. "We haven't a thing to give her," said Nellie.

"Here are some life savers," said Freddie. He pulled a half-opened package from his pocket and began to drop the candy one by one into the elephant's trunk.

"I'll pick some grass," said Nellie. "Maybe she'd like that."

Nan noted the heavy padlock on the back of the crate. "I'll ride to the nearest farmhouse and call the police," she said. "We must get Baby May out of that box before the thieves come back."

At that moment the curtain of willow branches was thrust aside. Nan gasped and the other children turned. Flossie's hand froze on the elephant's trunk.

"Baby May, are you in there?" Flossie called

The carnival man stood there! His eyes bugged out as he saw the children.

"Kids!" he croaked. "They're on to us! The deal's off!" He dropped the willow curtain and fled.

The children burst into laughter. "Oh, my knees are still shaking!" Nellie exclaimed.

"Was he scared!" said Freddie happily. "Did you see his face?"

"Now Baby May won't be sold and the bad men will be caught!" said Flossie.

"I'd better get the police right away," said Nan.

Flossie hugged the elephant's trunk. "You're saved, Baby May!"

As Nan turned to leave she gave a sudden scream. Two men had appeared suddenly. They popped into the front seat of the station wagon. The engine roared and the car shot off, dragging the crate behind it.

"They're getting away!" Freddie shouted. "Stop them!"

Frantically the children raced for their bicycles.

"We can't let them go!" cried Nan, leaping onto her bicycle. *"We just can't!"*

The children pedaled madly down the road with the crate bumping along ahead and Baby May's trunk still waving out the back. It drew farther and farther away.

"No use!" cried Nan. "We've lost them!"

CHAPTER XV

A MUDDY RESCUE

THE station wagon and crate disappeared around a bend. All the children stopped pedaling their bicycles and sadly wheeled them to the side of the road.

Flossie was crying, and there were tears in Nan's eyes. She put one arm around her little sister.

Freddie's lip quivered as he asked, "How will we ever find Baby May again?"

"You mustn't give up hope," said Nellie.

Nan quickly wiped her hand across her eyes. "Of course not. We're going to keep right on trying." She took a clean handkerchief from the pocket of her pedal pushers and dried Flossie's eyes. "Come now, keep your chin up."

Trying to be brave, the children rode home. Nellie said good-by at her house, and a few minutes later the Bobbseys arrived home.

Bert was in the living room with his mother and father. Quickly he said that the Milford clue had been a hoax.

"We know," Nan replied, "because we saw Baby May ourselves."

Her brother and parents looked astonished. Nan told the story.

"Did you get the license number?" Bert asked eagerly.

"We couldn't see the one on the station wagon," Nan replied, "and the crate didn't have any."

"The thieves must have bought a new car," said Mrs. Bobbsey. "The other one was black."

"Maybe they painted it green," Bert suggested.

Mr. Bobbsey telephoned a report to the police. He was told that the crate had been stolen from a farmer.

"What do you think the bad men will do with Baby May now?" Flossie asked.

Bert shrugged. "They may try to sell her again or they might just dump her some place."

"In the crate?" Flossie cried out. "She—she would starve!"

None of the children had much appetite for supper that night, and they had a hard time going to sleep. They kept wondering where Baby May was at this very moment. Was she speeding away from Lakeport? Or was she locked up somewhere, abandoned and hungry?

At breakfast next morning Nan pushed away

her toast and said, "I feel awful. The men got away with Baby May, and we've let Tippy down."

Bert called Chief Smith to see if they had had any leads to the photographer's sister.

"No," he said. "Sorry."

At school the twins tried to keep their minds on lessons, but they kept worrying about Tippy and Baby May. That afternoon the four walked home together.

"Poor Tippy," said Flossie. "She won't be able to take the trip or make her big picture book. And it's all our fault."

"Maybe we missed a clue somewhere," Nan said. "Think everybody—think *hard!*"

The children walked along in silence. Then suddenly Flossie had an idea.

"Maybe M's Mum—" she spoke up.

"What?" Freddie asked.

"M's Mum," his twin repeated carefully. "You know, the flower on the wall in Tippy's house."

As the other three stared at her, bewildered, Flossie explained about the prize flower. "Maybe M stands for Margery," she added.

Bert's face lit up. "It might be! Do you know who gave her the prize?"

Flossie thought of the writing she had seen underneath the chrysanthemum. "Vinton Botanical Gardens," she answered.

"Maybe the people there will know where Margery lives!" said Nan.

Excited, the twins raced home and told their mother the idea. Quickly Mrs. Bobbsey put away the sock she was mending and grabbed her purse from the hall table.

"Come on! We haven't a minute to waste!" She hurried to the garage with the children right behind her.

Vinton was a medium-sized town about twenty minutes from Lakeport. The Bobbseys had often been to the Botanical Gardens there.

As they entered the big greenhouse, the warm, moist air smelled of spring flowers. Nan led the way down a flagstone path toward a white-haired man digging beside a bush.

"Can you please tell us where the head gardener is?" she asked.

The man stood up and dusted his hands against his overalls. "You're speaking to him," he said.

Quickly the children's mother explained about the search for Margery.

The gardener smiled. "I remember. It was five years ago, but I'll never forget her flower. Biggest and best mum we ever had here!"

Bert spoke up eagerly. "Can you tell us where this lady lives?"

The man narrowed his eyes. "Well, it was a lake—Winona or Ramona. I'm not sure which."

"Do you know her last name?" Nan asked anxiously.

"No," was the reply. "All I remember is that everyone called her Margery."

Mrs. Bobbsey spoke up. "Is there an office here that could give us the information?"

"Yes, ma'am. But we don't bother to keep flower show records longer than three years."

"Let's call the Vinton newspaper," said Bert quickly. "They must have covered the event."

The gardener shook his head and said, "I'm afraid that's no use. There was a big fire at their office a couple of weeks ago. It burned up their file of old papers. Sorry I can't help you more."

"You've given us a good clue," Nan told him.

The Bobbseys thanked him and hurried out to the station wagon. Nan said, "I think we ought to try Lake Winona first. It's closest."

Her mother agreed. "Besides, Amy Scott lives there. She might be able to help us."

Mrs. Bobbsey went to a telephone booth on the corner and called her friend Mrs. Scott. "We'll be at your house in about half an hour," she said.

Mrs. Scott lived in a large white house on a shady street. She listened with interest to their story and examined the snapshot. But she had never seen Margery before.

"She may have a home on the lake shore," said Mrs. Scott. "That's some distance from town. I don't know many of those people. There was an excursion boat, but I can't recall the name of it."

"I guess we'll have to drive out and ask around," Mrs. Bobbsey said.

"The road is very bad," her friend replied. "They're doing a lot of work out at the lake and the rough parts won't be fixed until it's all finished."

"Maybe we can rent bikes," Bert proposed.

"Yes, do that!" Mrs. Scott said enthusiastically. "Suppose your mother stays here and visits with me."

Mrs. Bobbsey agreed and her friend directed the twins to a bicycle shop. In a short time the children were pedaling along a rutted road through the woods.

Finally they came out of the trees to a large open basin. The twins stopped in surprise.

"There's no water in the lake!" Flossie said.

Before them lay a vast expanse of weed-choked ground. It was strewn with soft-drink bottles, broken oars and rocks.

A nearby billboard informed the public that part of Lake Winona was to be the site of an outdoor swimming pool and bathers' pavilion. Until these were built, there would be no water in the lake.

In the distance the children could see an old boat which had been left in the mud. "Maybe it's the *Sea Sprite!*" Freddie exclaimed.

"No, it's not a launch," said Nan.

Her little brother was not listening. He

hopped off his bicycle and jumped from the road to the lake bed. Freddie began to run toward the stranded boat, but suddenly he gave a yell and stopped.

"Help!" he called, waving his arms wildly. "I'm sinking!" The more he struggled to free himself, the deeper his feet sank.

"Stand still, Freddie!" Bert shouted. "I'm coming!"

He spotted a wide board on the lake bottom a few feet from the edge. With Nan's help he managed to push it over the mud toward Freddie.

Then Bert crawled along the plank. Stretching out on his stomach, he grabbed Freddie's arm and pulled him onto the board. Inching backward he managed to get his little brother onto firmer ground. A few minutes later they both stood on the road.

"Freddie, you're a mess!" Nan exclaimed and Flossie giggled.

From the waist down, he was covered with black mud!

Freddie grinned. "I'm pretty dirty!" he admitted.

"What will we do?" Nan asked. "You can't go back to Mrs. Scott's looking like that!"

"There's a house," Flossie spoke up, looking through a grove of trees. It was a new-looking white building.

"Let's try it," said Nan. "Maybe those people

"Help! I'm sinking!"

will help us get Freddie clean. And we'll ask about Margery," she added.

As the children wheeled their bicycles up the driveway, they saw a large dark-haired man putting up a restaurant sign on the roof.

"We'd better go to the back door," Bert remarked with a grin.

A motherly-looking woman answered Bert's knock. "My sakes!" she exclaimed. "What happened to you?"

"I got stuck in the mud," said Freddie.

"We'd like to clean him up a little before we go back to town," Nan explained.

The woman pushed open the door. "Take off your shoes and come right in, sonny," she said. "My washer and dryer have just been connected. We'll have you clean in two shakes of a lamb's tail."

Bert went inside with Freddie to help him out of his clothes. A few minutes later they came out. Freddie was wearing a man's bathrobe. The sleeves had been rolled to his elbows and the middle had been pulled up over the sash so that it hung down to his knees.

Flossie giggled. "You look so funny!"

"I know," said Freddie, grinning.

The children waited, impatient to question the woman. Shortly she came out, saying, "I'm Mrs. Wilson. My husband and I are going to open a restaurant here as soon as the pool is finished. Would you like to come in and look around while the little boy's clothes are drying?"

Talking all the while, she led the Bobbseys through the front door and showed them a large dining room.

"The snack bar is next to it," she said and took them into a smaller room with a counter and stools along one side.

"This part is open now," she said. "Would you like a soda or something?"

"Thank you," said Nan. "I guess we are thirsty."

As the children took their places at the counter, they glanced at the mirror behind it. Over the top of the frame was a weathered-looking board.

On it were the words SEA SPRITE.

"That sign!" cried Nan as the others exclaimed in excitement.

"Where did it come from?" Bert asked. "Did the boat run on this lake?"

Mrs. Wilson looked proud. "Yes, it did. I got that board from the old excursion launch that used to take sightseers around the lake. When we open the new restaurant, I want people to feel at home," she explained.

"Then this is the right lake!" cried Flossie.

"Quick, Bert! Show Mrs. Wilson the photograph!" said Nan.

As her brother reached into his pocket, Nan happened to look into the mirror. She saw the outside door of the snack bar opening behind them.

With a cry of surprise, she bounded off the stool. All the children turned to look.

Their eyes opened wide in excitement!

CHAPTER XVI

BERT'S INVENTION

"TIPPY!" the children shouted. They ran forward and told her about winning the prize.

She stared at them amazed. "*I* won the prize? But I *couldn't* have!"

"You did, Tippy!" Nan insisted, squeezing the girl's hand. "You did!"

"It's true," cried Flossie happily, "but you have to go to New York right away to claim your prize!"

"By midnight tonight!" Freddie added.

Tippy's eyes filled with tears. "You wonderful children! You went to all this trouble to find me!" She hugged Nan and Flossie.

Bert said, "You'd better go now, Tippy. There's no time to waste!"

"Okay, I'll get the station wagon!" she said, dashing out. "I'll take you home first."

"What about Freddie?" asked Flossie. "He can't go in that bathrobe."

"His clothes must be dry by now," Mrs. Wilson put in quickly. She laughed. "My goodness, we don't usually have so much excitement around here."

Bert and Freddie followed her back through the restaurant to her living quarters. In a few minutes they returned with Freddie dressed in his own clothes.

Just then Tippy drove up. The children loaded their bicycles into the back and thanked Mrs. Wilson for her help. Then they took off with a roar. As they rode along, Bert gave Tippy back the photograph and explained why the Bobbseys had borrowed it.

Flossie asked if Tippy knew about Baby May. "Oh, yes," the girl replied. "I've been watching television, hoping for news that she'd been found."

Quickly the older twins told about their search for the elehpant.

"Don't be discouraged," the girl photographer said. "You'll find her. You're good detectives!" Then she added, "Could I help you?"

"As a matter of fact," said Bert, "I have a plan I'd like to try tomorrow after school, but I'd need a car for it."

"I'll drive you wherever you want to go," said Tippy. She explained that her sister had made a quick recovery and could be left alone now.

"Thanks a lot," said Bert. "That will be great."

Tippy laughed. "I'll be your assistant detective!"

When they reached Mrs. Scott's house, the red-haired girl parked and hurried inside with Nan. She was introduced to Mrs. Bobbsey's friend. Hugging the children's mother, Tippy said, "You and the twins were so wonderful to find me! I can't thank you enough!"

Meanwhile the others had unloaded the bicycles. Minutes later Tippy started off for New York.

After returning the bicycles, the Bobbseys went home. Everyone was thrilled at the children's success. Dinah gave them all extra big ice cream desserts.

"I'm mighty proud of my detectives," she said.

"Now if only we can find Baby May!" said Nan. Turning to her father, she added, "Bert has a plan, Daddy."

"I'd like to search the farmland again," her twin said.

"It's okay with me," his father agreed, "but I'm afraid you'll be disappointed."

A little later Bert went to the basement and soon the family heard sawing and hammering. Freddie went downstairs to watch.

"I have an idea, too," Flossie said to Nan. "Let's make a present for Baby May— something nice to give our elephant if we find her."

"Do you have an idea?" Nan asked. The little girl whispered into her sister's ear.

Nan laughed and said, "Come on! I'm sure Mother'll let us use her sewing machine."

Next day after school the girls changed to pedal pushers and sweaters while their brothers put on dungarees and T-shirts. Then they hurried to Tippy's house.

"Did you get the prize?" Flossie asked.

"Yes, thanks to you darlings. I just made it in time. I'll be taking the trip around the world. Now tell me what your plans are. You haven't found Baby May yet, have you?"

"No, but we're going to look again," Bert said. "That is, if you're sure you don't mind driving us."

"Glad to," Tippy said.

When they went outside Bert and Freddie showed her several coils of rope and a wooden fence-like structure they had laid on the ground. Flossie had a large cardboard box which she put into the station wagon.

Tippy looked at the things in amusement. "What is all this?"

"There's a present for Baby May in the box," Flossie told her. "It's a surprise. Nan and I brought it 'cause we want to show it to you after—" Flossie put her hand over her mouth. She was not going to give away any secrets!

Freddie spoke up. "And the wooden thing is a keen idea!" He bounced with excitement. "Bert's a real inventor!"

Bert grinned. "You may think it's cuckoo,

Tippy, but it's a lookout for us to find Baby May. Come on, Nan!"

The older twins scrambled to the roof. Tippy handed up the ropes and the wooden contraption. The two children lashed it securely in several places to the luggage rail. The fence was made of sturdy pieces of lumber and stood firm when they tested it.

"Nan and I will stand here and hold onto the rail," Bert explained. "Freddie and Flossie can kneel in the back and look out that way." He added that they would all be tied on tightly with ropes and Tippy would drive very slowly.

"Great idea!" said the photographer. "But where are we heading?" she asked as the twelve-year-olds jumped down from the roof.

"Across the drawbridge to the farmland," Bert replied.

"The police searched that area thoroughly," Tippy said.

"I know, but they probably inspected the buildings at each farm and asked about hiding places like deserted barns or sheds."

"That's right," said Tippy. "Police reported searching every abandoned building for miles."

Bert reminded her that the farmland was hilly. "There could be a house or barn behind a rise of ground—a place you couldn't see from the road."

"That's right," said Nan, eager to get going. Everyone got into the station wagon and

Tippy started off. They rode through town, along River Road, past factories and over the drawbridge.

When they reached the top of the hill, Bert said, "Now let's get on the roof."

They all hopped out. The twins climbed up to the enclosure. When Freddie and Flossie were fastened securely, Bert and Nan put ropes around their own waists and tied the ends to the fence.

"Hold onto the luggage rack, Freddie and Flossie, in case we go over a bump," said Nan.

Tippy slipped behind the wheel. When Bert heard the car door slam, he called, "Okay, let 'er roll!"

The station wagon crept forward. From their high perch the twins could see for miles across the green, rolling land. Now and then a car passed and the children waved at the amazed drivers.

Suddenly Nan called, "Stop!"

The car halted. Tippy's head came out of the window. "See something?"

"Yes," said Nan. She pointed to her right across a meadow. "I see a valley over there and the tip of a roof."

"I don't see anything," said Bert.

"We've moved a little bit since then," said Nan, "and now a tree is in the way."

"We'd better have a look!" called Tippy. She drove the car off the road and parked.

As Nan and Bert were untying themselves, there came a sudden yell from Freddie, and Flossie cried out, "Come quick!"

The older twins made their way to the back of the roof. Freddie was dangling a few feet over the ground on his rope!

"He was so 'cited he forgot to untie himself," and Flossie.

Tippy came running and held the little boy up while Nan and Bert removed his rope. Then she set him on the ground.

Quickly Flossie untied herself. As Tippy helped her down, the older children followed.

Nan spoke to Freddie sternly. "You must be more careful. Detectives look before they leap."

In spite of himself, Bert grinned. "I guess Freddie was at the end of his rope." The girls laughed and even Freddie chuckled.

The twins started across the meadow with Tippy. It rose gently toward the rim of the valley. Nearby, Nan spotted the ruts of an old wagon road. The searchers followed it to the top of the rise and looked down.

At the foot of a steep slope was a barn, black with age. A big tree growing out of the hillside almost hid a gaping hole in the roof. Some distance off, amid high grass, was the burned-out foundation of a farmhouse.

"I'll bet this place has been forgotten for years," said Bert.

They looked carefully over the abandoned

"Come quick!" cried Flossie

property. There was no sign of the two men, the brown crate, or the station wagon. Bert turned and scanned the field behind them. At the edge of it, about quarter of a mile down the road, was a large grove of oaks.

"The car and crate could be hidden there," Bert said softly.

"Let's try the barn first," Nan suggested.

Cautiously the five made their way down the hill. At the bottom they stopped by the side of the barn and listened. All was still.

Tippy looked up the steep slope and shook her head doubtfully. "It would be a very hard place to bring an elephant," she whispered. "Besides—"

Before she could finish the sentence, a thin trumpeting came from inside the barn!

CHAPTER XVII

A SHAKY PERCH

"IT'S Baby May!" whispered Flossie, tingling with excitement.

"The question is," said Bert, "are the men in there with her?"

Though the barn was old, the heavy timbers were close set. The twins and Tippy saw no crack or knothole through which they could peek.

Quietly they walked through the weeds to the front of the building. The wide door was secured by a heavy wooden bar. Above it was a padlock.

"The bad men are gone," said Freddie. "They locked Baby May in and went off some place."

Bert suggested that Tippy drive to the nearest farmhouse and call the police. "We'll stay here and keep an eye on the barn."

"No," Tippy decided. "It's too dangerous. The men might come back."

"Then we'll hide," Nan said.

"Let us stay here, Tippy," Bert pleaded. "If they try to take Baby May away, we might be able to delay them."

"Or find out where they're going," Freddie spoke up.

"All right," Tippy said, "but whatever you do, promise to hide if they come."

The children agreed. As the photographer hurried up the slope, the elephant trumpeted again.

"She sounds so lonesome, I wish we could go in and see her," said Flossie. The animal's noise grew louder and Bert looked around uneasily.

"I'd like to quiet her," he said. "If the men come back and hear her making a fuss, they might suspect something's up."

"Maybe we can find a loose board and sneak in," Freddie suggested. The twins walked around the side and the back of the barn, but saw no opening.

Suddenly Bert snapped his fingers. "Maybe the roof!"

He scrambled up the hill with the others at his heels. When they reached a tree, Bert jumped for a low limb and swung himself onto it. After helping the others up, he crawled out on a stout branch which hung over the hole in the roof.

Bert carefully let himself down onto the old shingles. Looking through the opening, he saw a hayloft.

"We'll go in this way," he called. "When I give the signal, you come."

"Right," replied Nan. She guided Flossie and Freddie ahead of her onto the limb.

Meanwhile, Bert grasped the side of the hole and lowered himself through it. He dropped into a large pile of old hay.

Crack! The floor of the loft moved!

"Come on!" Bert called up.

Nan's face appeared at the opening and she helped Flossie to climb through it. Bert grasped his little sister and lowered her gently onto the hay.

"Take it easy," he warned. "This loft is kind of shaky."

Freddie was lowered next, and then Nan followed. The twins made their way across the hay to the edge of the loft. Below they saw Baby May! She was tethered to a stout post with a heavy leather thong.

Seeing them, the little elephant set up a shrill trumpeting. She began to dance.

"We're coming, Baby May!" Flossie called and stepped toward a wooden ladder which led to the floor of the barn.

"Hold it!" Bert said sharply. "That looks rickety. Better let me go first."

Gingerly he descended. At the bottom he called up, "Watch out. Those rungs won't take much."

He held the ladder steady as Flossie started

down. "This isn't nailed in place," he told the others. "It's only propped here."

One by one, the twins made their way carefully to the floor. Then Freddie started quickly toward the little elephant.

Nan caught him back. "Not so fast," she warned. "If you excite her, she might accidentally hurt you. After all, she's a heavy animal."

"That's right," Bert agreed. "It's not the same as hugging our dog Snap."

As the children walked up to the crying elephant, Nan talked softly to her. Baby May put out her trunk and the children took it gently. The animal grew calmer, and soon the twins were stroking her.

Bert looked over the loft and saw that two of the supporting posts were split and rotten. "We were lucky to get down here safely," he said.

Underneath the loft was a great mound of old straw. In a corner was a small bale of fresh hay.

"I'll bet Baby May's hungry," said Flossie and ran over to get some.

As she and Freddie began to feed the elephant, Nan picked up the toy bag which lay at the animal's feet.

For an instant Baby May's eyes opened wide and she looked at the older twins. Then she dropped her lids and went on munching hay.

Nan reached inside the bag and pulled out the brown cloth sack. The bluish-green box was in it.

"Is the cup inside?" Bert asked.

"Yes. All safe."

At that moment came a loud click! *Someone was opening the padlock!*

The young twins dropped the hay, darted to the ladder and climbed swiftly to the loft. Nan was right behind them, carrying the brown sack. Bert quickly closed the toy bag and put it into place.

"Hurry, hurry!" Nan whispered as her brother started up the ladder.

The twins heard the heavy bar being lifted off the door and the loud squeak of the hinges as it opened. Bert was about to crawl onto the loft when the rung he was standing on broke!

Stifling an outcry, he clung to the edge of the loft, his legs thrashing. As the wooden platform trembled, the others reached to help him. The thieves entered and walked toward the loft.

"They'll see Bert!" Nan thought wildly.

But the men went straight to the elephant without an upward glance. By the time they were directly below, Bert had scrambled to safety.

The children burrowed into the hay close to the edge and peered down. Covering himself, Freddie saw that he had just missed lying on a couple of pigeon eggs. He made a face, wondering how long ago they had been laid there.

As the thieves stepped closer to Baby May, she swooped up her bag of toys and put it between her front legs. Swinging her trunk back

"They'll see Bert!" Nan thought wildly

and forth, she watched the men from under her lashes.

Crow rubbed his hands together. "This is our lucky day, Lester!" he exclaimed. "I told you I'd get a buyer for that cup and I've done it!" He glanced at his watch. "In just one hour we'll be in that collector's house. He'll hand over a nice fat check and we'll hand over the loot." Then Crow added sharply, "Hurry up now! Get out the cup."

"Get it yourself!" Lester retorted. "It was your idea to put it back in the bag."

Crow replied, "That's the safest hiding place I know."

"It's not so safe for the one who has to get the cup out," his companion grumbled. "Every time I go for that bag, she swats me with her trunk. I'm getting tired of it."

"Stop complaining," Crow snapped. "If it hadn't been for me, we wouldn't have the loot. Who learned about the elephant coming to America? Who found out that she would carry the bag of toys with her? Who stole the cup from the museum? I did!" he declared. "All you had to do was hide in that Thailand zoo, jimmy open that fancy elephant house and put the loot with the toys. It came out of Thailand and into this country just as I planned. We never had a bit of trouble!"

"But we've had plenty ever since," said Lester bitterly. "Once that beast got to America, she wouldn't part with the sack. Remember the airport? She kicked up so much fuss that everyone thought we were trying to kidnap *her!*"

"Don't blame me," said Crow. "How was I to know that the animal would get violent over the bag? She didn't act that way in Bangkok."

"Now we're stuck with an elephant," Lester grumbled.

"Too bad," said his partner, "but there was no other way."

"It hasn't been easy!" exclaimed the small man angrily. "Who tramped through the woods looking for a place to hide that animal? Who found the shack? Who tried to take the bag away from her there? I did! And I'm the one she knocked down when she broke out!"

"The trouble with you," said Crow, "is that you're afraid of the elephant."

Lester sneered. "I guess you're not!"

"You'll feel different about it," remarked Crow, "when we sell her to a carnival for a lot of money."

The small man groaned. "I wish you'd forget about that. I'm fed up with the elephant. I say get rid of her!"

"Now listen, Lester," his partner said smoothly, "I admit that things haven't gone exactly as I planned, but most of our troubles were due to those Bobbsey twins."

Hardly daring to breathe, the children listened as Lester replied, "When we heard them talking by that willow tree, I was ready to settle their hash then and there. You should have let me do it!"

"Don't worry," said Crow. "If they turn up again I'll teach 'em a lesson myself." Then he added briskly, "Now get that bag. We're wasting time!"

The twins watched tensely as Lester took a step forward, then paused. Baby May's trunk curled around the bag and she lifted it a few inches from the floor.

Lester held out his hand cautiously. "Nice elephant!" As he dived for the bag, Baby May flung it under her body and sat down on it!

Crow let out a cry of dismay. "No! Stop her! She's crushing the cup!"

"She's never done that before," said Lester feebly.

"Make her get up!" replied his partner furiously. "Get up! Get up!" he shouted at the elephant.

Lester pushed at the animal's sides, but Baby May sat firm. Crow looked around frantically. Seeing an old rake in a corner of the barn, he hurried over, picked it up and carried it back to the elephant.

The children had watched, wide-eyed, trying to hold back nervous giggles, but when they saw Crow's face, their hearts sank. He was dark red with fury! Raising the rake handle high over Baby May's trunk, he shouted, "I'll get her up!"

Nan covered her eyes and Freddie winced. As he did, his elbow knocked an egg off the loft.

Smack! It broke right on top of Crow's head!

With a cry the man dropped the rake handle and clutched his hair. "Phooey!" he cried as the smeary stuff came down over his face. He yanked a handkerchief from his pocket and wiped his head and hands.

As soon as the egg had dropped, the children had backed deeper into the hay. Bert, who was close to the ladder, saw the two men look up.

"There must be someone in the loft," Crow muttered.

"Aw, it's nothing," said Lester. "A mouse, maybe."

Crow's voice was cold and hard. "I'm going to see." He stepped toward the ladder!

CHAPTER XVIII

THE ELEPHANT'S TRICKS

THE twins were trapped! Then suddenly Bert reached down and jerked up the ladder.

Crow leaped for it with a cry of rage, but just missed the bottom rung. Quickly the other children threw off the hay and helped their brother pull the ladder onto the shaking loft.

"I knew it!" Crow shouted. "The twins again!"

Lester stared up at them open-mouthed. Then he turned on his partner. "I told you to get rid of that elephant and the station wagon, too! But you wouldn't! You said all we needed to be safe was a coat of green paint on the car and new license plates! Now look what's happened!"

"It's all your fault!" Crow retorted. "Why didn't you keep watch outside the way I did at the factory? We got away that night because I saw those kids coming and gave you the alarm."

The twins, still trembling from their narrow escape, listened as the thieves quarreled.

"I'd like to know how they ever spotted this place," said Crow. "We'd never have found it ourselves if I hadn't made you climb a tree and look for a hideout with your binoculars."

"Never mind all that! What'll we do now?" Lester asked angrily. Crow glared up at the children a moment, then whispered something in his partner's ear and strode out of the barn.

Lester stepped gingerly to the elephant. "Get up, you!" he said harshly. He kicked Baby May in the side and then ran backwards quickly.

The twins shouted at him to stop. "You ought to be ashamed of yourself!" Nan declared.

Lester's eyes narrowed. "Too bad you couldn't take a hint," he said unpleasantly. "When Crow and I were leaving Big Pine Lake after locking up that dancer, we caught sight of you on a dock. I was afraid you would hear about the fellow being missing and start looking for him, so—"

"You dumped our bikes in the lake!" exclaimed Bert.

"That's right," said Lester. "We did it to show that you had enemies at the lake. I hoped you'd be afraid and go home." The thief shook his head. "But you never give up."

"Now you'll be sorry!" came a deep voice from above. Crow's angry face was peering through the hole in the roof!

"Don't jump!" Bert cried. "It isn't safe!"

But the big man leaped.

CRASH!

"Now you'll be sorry!" Crow growled

Straight through the rickety floor he went and down came the loft with twins, eggs and hay!

Crow yelled and the children screamed, but no one was hurt, because all of them had landed on the pile of straw underneath. As Nan hit, however, the brown cup bag flew from her hand. She scrambled to her feet, but Lester grabbed the bag and ran for the door.

"Come on!" he yelled to Crow. "Forget the kids and the elephant!"

The tall man leaped up and bounded after his partner. Together they dashed through the door and slammed it shut. As the children hurled themselves against it, they heard the bar drop into place with a thud.

"Oh, no!" Flossie wailed. "They're stealing the cup again!"

"We must get out of here!" cried Bert.

Nan dashed back and untied Baby May. "You're going to help us," she told the elephant.

She grabbed the bag of toys and led the elephant to the door. Bert was pushing on a board.

"This one's a little loose. Maybe she could knock it out."

"Sure!" Freddie exclaimed. "Get her baseball bat, quick!"

"Wait!" his brother said. He ran across the barn and brought back a two-by-four piece of lumber. "This is heavier." He held it out, and the elephant took it in her trunk.

Bert stepped aside and patted the place beside

the door. "Okay, Baby May, put it there—a home run!"

The elephant swung the piece of lumber hard against the board. It moved a little. Once more—WHAM! The timber broke outward several inches.

As the children praised the elephant, she dropped the board and slipped her trunk through the opening.

"Good girl!" cried Nan. "Raise the bar!" A moment later the twins heard the scrape of wood. Bert pushed the door open and burst out, followed by the other children and the elephant.

The thieves were scrambling over the top of the slope. Baby May waved her trunk in the air and caught their scent. She trumpeted loudly and charged up the hill with the twins.

Startled, Lester looked back, tripped and fell. The brown bag sailed out of his hand and landed in the high grass.

"The cup!" he shouted. "I've lost it!"

Crow dashed back, and the two men pawed frantically through the weeds. By the time the bag was found, the Bobbseys had nearly reached them.

The thieves raced across the meadow. Right behind them came Baby May with her trunk upended. Her eyes glittered angrily.

Bert ran beside her with Nan clutching the toy bag. Freddie and Flossie were close behind.

When the men reached the grove of trees, they

leaped over a brook. Together they dashed to their station wagon, which was parked with the crate under a big oak.

"Stop them!" cried Freddie as the children jumped the brook.

Baby May splashed through and thundered straight at the thieves. They cried out in fear and darted around the crate. Desperately, Crow threw himself onto the hood of the station wagon. From there he scrambled up into the low branches of the oak. Lester joined him. Baby May stood at the foot of the tree, waving her trunk, and trumpeting.

"That's right, keep 'em up there!" Bert exclaimed. "Flossie and Freddie, run out to the road and tell Tippy where we are when she comes with the police."

The men threatened and pleaded until the young twins were heard shouting from the road. Then Tippy's station wagon thumped into the grove followed by a black squad car with Officers Lane, Brown, and Denver. In minutes they reached the twins and jumped out.

Officer Lane asked, "Where are the thieves?"

All the children pointed into the tree and the policemen had to smile.

"Move that elephant away," Officer Brown said to the twins. "We'll get them down."

Nan led Baby May past the police car to the brook. While the animal drank thirstily, the policemen made Crow and Lester come down out of the tree. Officer Denver took possession of the cup.

"You two thought you were pretty smart," he said to the thieves. "But you're going to end up in jail."

Lester was pale. "I'll be glad to go to jail to get away from that elephant!"

"And those twins," added Crow bitterly.

Officer Lane asked what had happened. Quickly Bert told their story. The three policemen praised the children warmly.

"You're great detectives," said Officer Lane.

Then he and the others put the thieves into the back seat of the police car. At the same time Baby May took a trunkful of water, and squirted it through the open window onto her captors.

"A farewell shower!" said Bert with a chuckle as the car pulled away.

Officer Denver remained behind to drive the green station wagon. The children helped him load the elephant into the crate.

"Don't be afraid, honey," Flossie called in to her. "We'll see you at the zoo."

Half an hour later both cars drove up to the front entrance where a crowd was waiting. The story had been radioed ahead by the police and the news had spread. Flashbulbs of photographers popped. Television cameras covered the scene as Mr. Burns shook hands with the Bobbseys.

"Everyone wants to hear your story," he said, "so I've suggested that the TV cameras be set up at our circus ring. We'll have more room there."

Walking beside the manager and Tippy, the twins led Baby May into the zoo. The crowd followed. Nan carried the toy bag, Tippy her camera, and Flossie clutched Baby May's surprise.

Keeper Henry was waiting inside one of the sawdust circus rings. He had a pail of milk for Baby May and a mound of fresh hay. At once the elephant stepped over the side of the ring and walked to her refreshments.

While she munched, a friendly young newscaster questioned the twins. Modestly Bert told about rescuing the elephant and the cup.

The newsman told them that the story had been telephoned to the Thailand Embassy in Washington. "Officials there say that each of you will be rewarded with a small gold elephant."

"I'd like to give something to these children, too," Mr. Burns spoke up. "Is there anything you Bobbseys especially want?"

Nan said, "I'd like Baby May to have a nice red house with a curvy gold roof like her home in Thailand." The other twins agreed quickly.

"She shall have it!" declared the zoo manager.

Just then Danny Rugg and his pal Jack elbowed their way to the edge of the ring.

"That's a dopey elephant," said Danny loudly and looked around with a grin, hoping everyone had heard him.

"She never does any tricks," Jack added.

"She knows *lots* of tricks," Flossie declared.

Danny sneered. "Oh yeah?"

Nan flushed. "I'll show you."

She took all of Baby May's toys from the bag and laid them on the ground in a row. Flossie brought the elephant to the center of the ring.

Nan began to make the various sounds that Thiang had taught her. After each signal Baby May did a trick. First she rang her bell. Then she rocked the cloth doll in her trunk. Next the animal picked up the ivory-handled brush and carefully brushed off Freddie's shirt.

"Now she'll do her first American trick," Bert announced. Baby May hit a home run with her ball and bat. As the audience laughed and clapped, Danny and Jack slunk away.

Meanwhile, the two girls opened the cardboard box.

"We have a present for the elephant!" Flossie announced.

She held up a big white baby bonnet with pink ribbons on it. Speaking softly to the animal, she and Nan placed the frilly cap on her head and tied the wide ribbons under her chin. Then Flossie took an empty baby bottle from the box.

"I'll give you some milk for that!" called Keeper Henry.

Flossie ran over with the bottle and filled it. Then she handed the bottle to Baby May. The elephant curled the tip of her trunk around the bottle and held it.

"Now, Baby May," said Nan gently, "listen!"

The girl gave three little chirps and one long whistle. At that, Baby May sat up straight on her hind quarters, raised her front feet and held the bottle high in the air.

As the audience applauded, Freddie and Bert came over laughing. Tippy snapped the picture.

"That'll be the first one in my big book!" she called to the twins.

The newscaster praised the girls for the cute idea. "Why did you decide to give the elephant from Thailand an American-style bonnet?" he asked.

"Because she's an American baby now," said Flossie with a smile.